"Well, Well . . . What Have We Here?

"Don't tell me a little ol' flat tire got you stranded in the wilds of East Texas!"

As if his mocking tone was more than she could take, Brittany twisted her head and said, "Don't you dare say it!"

"Say what?" He grinned and leaned against her car. "Say that I told you so?"

She lifted her chin slightly. "Go ahead, have your fun. But the last laugh will be on me. You'll see."

He crossed his arms over his chest and stared at her. "Oh, and just how do you figure that? Seems to me, I can fix your flat or choose to let you sit here and fume."

Brittany looked alarmed. "You wouldn't. It'll . . . it'll soon be dark," she added on a plaintive note.

"Well . . . then say the magic word."

"And just what is that?"

A display of innocence widened his eyes. "If you don't know, then I guess I'll be on my way. Too bad you can't join me."

"Don't you dare walk away from me!"

He kept on walking.

"All right!"

He slowly turned around and waited.

Dear Reader,

Happy holidays! At this busy time of year, I think it's extra important for you to take some time out for yourself. And what better way to get away from all the hustle and bustle of the season than to curl up somewhere with a Silhouette Desire novel? In addition, these books can make great gifts. Celebrate this season by giving the gift of love!

To get yourself in the holiday spirit, you should start with Lass Small's delightful *Man of the Month* book, *'Twas the Night*. Our hero has a plain name—Bob Brown—but as you fans of Lass Small all know, this will be no plain story. It's whimsical fun that only Lass can create.

The rest of December's lineup is equally wonderful. First, popular author Mary Lynn Baxter brings us a sexy, emotional love story, *Marriage, Diamond Style*. This is a book you'll want to keep. Next, Justine Davis makes her Silhouette Desire debut with *Angel for Hire*. The hero of this very special story is a *real* angel. The month is completed with stellar books by Jackie Merritt, Donna Carlisle and Peggy Moreland—winners all!

So go wild with Desire, and have a *wonderful* holiday season.

All the best,

Lucia Macro
Senior Editor

MARY LYNN BAXTER

MARRIAGE, DIAMOND STYLE

SILHOUETTE *Desire*®

Published by Silhouette Books New York

America's Publisher of Contemporary Romance

SILHOUETTE BOOKS
300 East 42nd St., New York, N.Y. 10017

MARRIAGE, DIAMOND STYLE

ISBN: 0-373-05679-6

First Silhouette Books printing December 1991

Printed in the U.S.A.

MARY LYNN BAXTER

sold hundreds of romances before she ever wrote one. The D & B Bookstore, right on the main drag in Lufkin, Texas, is the bookstore she owns and manages with her husband, Leonard, and her mother, Agnes Durham. D & B specializes in—what else?—romances and bestselling fiction. For relaxation, Mary Lynn and Leonard garden. Around five o'clock every evening they can be found picking butter beans on their small farm just outside of town.

Special thanks to Will Medlin,
for sharing his logging expertise

One

_____

The mosquito was big and ugly. And it was feasting on Matthew Diamond's leatherlike flesh.

"Why, you little s.o.b.," he muttered, and slapped his arm. He brushed off the offensive insect, along with a spot of blood, and kept on walking.

Mosquitoes were as much a part of East Texas as the equally offensive fire ants. While he detested both, he'd learned to live with them because the piney woods were where he lived and where he hoped to die.

The early morning air was cool and fresh. It stung Matt's face as he paused, looked toward the sky and took a deep breath. The dog at his heels stopped beside him and stared with adoration at his tall, lean master.

He returned the animal's stare with a smile. The large black mutt had wandered up to Matt's front porch one day and hadn't budged since.

Matt reckoned someone had dumped him on the highway and kept on going. At first he'd considered hauling the dog to the pound in Lufkin, but when Sam had whined that special whine of his and licked his hand, Matt had been lost. Anyway, he'd known he could use the company.

"Well, Sam, the weather's finally decided to cooperate."

Matt felt Sam's warm, slobbery tongue on the back of his hand.

"None too soon, wouldn't you say? Much more rain—and the loggers here will soon be history."

The licks turned damp and desperate before Matt scratched behind one of the animal's floppy ears.

"Only we both know the bad weather's only a small part of my problems. Right?"

This time Sam whined.

Matt shoved his Stetson back on his head and said, "Ah, come on, boy, you gotta think positive."

So did he. Today was going to be his lucky day. Yep, things were about to take a turn for the better. He could feel it in his bones.

When the dog didn't respond, Matt sighed. If his luck *didn't* change, he was in jeopardy of losing his logging business—a venture he'd put his heart and soul into, not to mention every penny he had.

Matt removed his hat and threaded his hands through sandy-blond hair that the summer sun had turned almost white. Before replacing the battered Stetson, he slapped another mosquito off his thigh.

"Come on, fellow, we'd best get going. Standing here lollygagging around isn't going to get it done." He smiled ruefully. "It's only going to get us eaten alive."

Ordinarily Matt would have been in the woods, set up and waiting for dawn in order to cut that first tree. But today he'd let his crew off so he could get in working order what little equipment he had left.

Now, as he made his way to the edge of the woods, to the shop where he kept and worked on the logging machinery, his gait was no longer a swagger. His troubled thoughts had dimmed the new day.

Sam seemed aware of Matt's mood change. He whined again and nuzzled Matt's hand.

"Yeah, I know, life's a bitch."

Only that hadn't always been the case. Until this latest round of rotten luck, life had been on an even keel. At age thirty-five, and for the first time ever, Matt was where he wanted to be, doing what he wanted to do.

A runaway at the age of sixteen, he couldn't think of a time when he wasn't fending for himself. His mother had handed him over to a church home shortly after he was born. Years of enduring foster homes had followed. The day he'd turned eighteen, he'd gone to work for an oil company for low pay. But it hadn't been long before he'd proved his worth. His reward had been a job in the oil fields in the Middle East.

Matt had liked what he did, especially the money, but he'd longed for roots, a place to call his own. So after years of desert heat, he returned to East Texas for good.

He bought a house on several acres of land and went into the logging business. His experience in that particular field was limited, but that didn't stop him. As a teenager he'd done some summer work for a logger and had enjoyed it.

Though the hours in the woods were long, grueling and sometimes dangerous, he couldn't think of another place he'd rather be. Making a success of his business was his top priority. His determination had earned him respect in the community.

There were difficult times, though. The loneliness that greeted him at the end of each day was almost unbearable. Since he refused to indulge himself, he pushed aside thoughts that he ought to be married with a couple of kids. He knew no woman would put up with his stubborn pride and his penchant for work.

Therefore, he'd convinced himself he was content, if not happy, with his lot in life. He was beginning to enjoy the fruits of his hard labor—then the first unexpected setback came. An accident in the woods claimed the life of one of his employees, a young man who was married and had a small child.

Matt's troubles hadn't ended there. Shortly afterward, his equipment woes had begun.

"Hey, boss, wait up."

Matt stopped in his tracks, turned and watched as his right-hand man, Elmer Cayhill, worked hard to catch up with him. He was a bear of a man with a distended waistline, head full of premature gray hair, face full of whiskers and skin the color of toasted almonds from too much exposure to the sun. Despite his physical imperfections, he was good-natured and could outwork any twenty-year-old.

Still, from where Elmer stood, Matt could hear his labored breathing and it worried him.

"If you don't get rid of that gut, my friend—"

"I know," Elmer cut in, finally reaching Matt's side. "You're gonna be picking me up in the woods and carting me to the morgue."

"Something like that."

Elmer snorted. "Seems to me I've heard that before."

"And you still haven't done a damn thing about it."

Elmer's well-fed face tightened. "What's more, I'm not gonna. If I can't have my beer, then I'll take the morgue."

Matt winced. "You're hopeless."

Elmer grinned. "So I'm told."

They walked in silence, the dog between them, his tail wagging nonstop.

"You didn't stop by to discuss your health," Matt said at last. It wasn't a question, but rather a statement.

"No, I didn't."

It wasn't so much what Elmer said but the way he said it that put Matt on instant guard. "More trouble?"

"'Fraid so."

Matt muttered an expletive.

"Yep, I'm afraid we've lost another one."

Matt cursed again. "Which one?"

Elmer shoved back the soiled baseball cap he wore and wiped his forehead, leaving a streak of grease across his face.

If the situation hadn't been so serious, Matt might have laughed. But the situation was far too serious. It was downright catastrophic.

"The big skidder."

A groan split Matt's lips. "Stolen?"

"No."

"Fire?"

"Yep."

"Damn!" Matt said, his eyes hot with anger.

"Burned to a crisp this time."

Matt shouldn't have been surprised. He should be well beyond that threshold. He should've conditioned himself to expect the worst. But he hadn't, and every time something went wrong, he felt the punch all over again.

Cayhill massaged the nest of whiskers on his chin, then spoke in an even tone, as if he suspected Matt couldn't take much more. "I guess it's a good thing I left my lunch bucket by that big oak tree. The wife sent me to get it, said anything I didn't eat would be stinking so that she'd have to throw the gall-darn thing away. So I went out at dawn to get it. The rest you know."

"Was there anything missing?"

"Not that I could tell."

"Dammit, Elmer, what's going on?" Matt asked, bitterly. "First a skidder caught on fire. Next, one was vandalized. Then a loader was stolen, and now another skidder caught on fire."

"At this rate, you can't keep on going, can you?"

Matt's laugh was hollow. "That's an understatement. I'm down to one skidder and loader and two trucks. How long do you think I can pay my bills with that piddling amount of equipment?"

"Not long."

Matt didn't reply. He didn't have to. His face said it all.

"What are you going to do?" Elmer's eyes were watchful.

"If something doesn't give, I'm going to be out of business."

"After we get the old standby running again," Elmer said quickly, "how 'bout I check with Ludlum and see if he's had any trouble with his equipment?"

Matt rubbed his neck; his muscles knotted under his hand. "Can't hurt, I guess, but you know how vocal he is. If the same thing had happened to him, we'd have heard him bellyaching already."

"So what are you saying?"

Matt squirmed as he looked into the distance for answers. "I don't know. That's just it. I don't know what the hell to think."

"Well, for starters, I guess you'd best call the sheriff."

"We both know that's a waste of time."

Elmer's smile was economical. "Couldn't agree with you more. I've always said that 'bout ol' Rex James. But for now, he's the best we got. And for the sake of your insurance, you have to call him."

Matt's spine stiffened. "Speaking of insurance, I've got to call them, too."

"Now that's the real kicker," Elmer drawled. "Think they'll give you trouble?"

"It's as certain as death and taxes," Matt said, biting back his disgust.

"They can't cancel you, can they?"

"No, at least not right now. But it won't stop them from sending a 'dress for success' down here to snoop around."

Elmer chuckled. "Mm, I like that. Anyway, you'd best get it over with."

Matt's shoulders sagged. He felt a weight, like an anvil, on his chest. "Yeah, I'd best get it over with."

He turned and trudged wearily toward the house.

Two

Glass was the focal point of Brittany Fleming's office. She twisted in her cushioned chair and took advantage of the view. On the buildings across the street, sunlight painted weird shadows.

The insurance company, one of the many businesses her daddy owned, occupied the top floor of the handsomely decorated office complex in downtown Tyler. It was the kind of building that caught one's eye because of its unusual and costly elegance.

But inside, Brittany's personal flair made the space her own. Most of the furniture was walnut. Walls and carpet were bright and vivid. Potted ficus trees and a small eucalyptus stood in a random pattern around the room, refreshing the air. Paintings further livened the space and made it cheerful without being frivolous.

She had worked hard to make a place for herself in Walter Fleming's financial empire, and though she was pleased with her progress thus far, she knew she had a long way to go.

Being the only child of a widowed insurance magnate was not easy, despite the fact that Brittany was beautiful, intelligent and had a body most models would die for. But there was another side of her. She was headstrong, spoiled and thought that because she was daddy's darling, the world was her oyster.

Yet she wanted to please her daddy, ached for his love instead of the things he had always given her.

She graduated with honors from college, then went to work for his company with two goals in mind—to gain Walter's recognition and respect and to prove she could hack it in a man's world.

On both counts, her expectations had fallen short. She was given only token jobs—and only because she was the owner's daughter. She was determined to correct that, however, beginning today.

Where her daddy was concerned ... well, their personal relationship was a different matter altogether. It was still on shaky ground, and she was no closer to accomplishing her goal.

Brittany blinked against the sudden and dazzling sunlight that streamed through the glass, and she realized she had tears in her eyes. Furious with the direction her thoughts had taken, she turned and focused her attention once again on Matthew Diamond's file. Her concentration had been severely damaged. Thinking about her daddy did it every time and never failed to reconstruct a memory best forgotten.

She'd been in the third grade and had worked extra hard to make a perfect straight A report card. One B on the previous card had earned a scolding from her daddy. On the day she had received that perfect record, she'd ridden home with her best friend, Sally. Sally had also made a perfect card, and when her mother saw it, she'd grabbed Sally, hugged and kissed her.

Brittany had watched from a distance and wished she had a mother like Sally's. But her mother had died when she was five. She'd had to depend on her daddy.

When Walter arrived home later that day, she raced into his office flapping her report in the air. "Daddy, Daddy!" she cried, her red curls bouncing around her cheeks. "I did it."

"Did what?" he asked absently.

"I got straight *A*s." Her eyes shone as she waited in anticipation at his side, aching for him to hug her and kiss her just like Sally's mom had done to her child.

He did neither. Instead, he patted her on the head and said, "Wonderful. Tell Benson to drive you into town and let you buy anything you want."

With those words, the light had gone out of her day. Brittany had wanted to cry, only she hadn't. But she remembered her heart had throbbed until she'd thought it would burst through her small chest.

The same way it felt now. "You're sick, Brittany Fleming," she spat aloud. "Why do you do this to yourself?"

So what if Walter couldn't show his affection? He loved her; he just didn't know how to show it. That was all. For God's sake, she was twenty-five years old. It was past time she grew up.

Brittany dabbed her eyes with a tissue, then turned her attention to her work. After a minute, her mind was again on track, but that didn't stop a frown from marring her brow. Why, this man was a menace, she thought. If the company had many more clients like him, they'd be out of business in no time. Something had to be done about him, and the sooner the better.

And she had the answer—to both problems. She would convince her immediate boss that she could handle this case. Pushing away from her desk, Brittany stood, her back rigid, as if prepared for battle.

Armed with her file and notes, she walked to the door. The phone halted her mid-stride.

"Great," she muttered, remembering that her secretary was out of the office today.

"Yes." Her agitation showed in her short response.

"Brittany?"

"Oh, hi, Howard." She perched on the edge of the desk and stifled a sigh.

Next to her daddy, Howard Hickman was the man she cared most about, but not enough to marry him, much to Howard's disappointment, as well as Walter's. He thought Howard was perfect for her. Perhaps he was. Though born into an old, moneyed family, he was successful in his own right. He had gained an outstanding reputation as a trial attorney. Besides that, he was good-looking.

She visualized him as he sat at his desk. His features were those of an inbred aristocrat. He parted his dark hair straight down the middle and sprayed it so it wouldn't move. His forehead was high, his eyes deeply set and his mouth thin, almost prim.

She wished she loved him; she wished she wanted to get married. Only she didn't. She had decided long ago that marriage wasn't for her, mainly because she had never found a man exciting enough or interesting enough to make her give up her independence.

At this point in her life, she wanted to concentrate on learning everything she could about the insurance business. Secretly, she had visions of running the company one day with her father's glowing approval.

"Brittany? You still there?"

She cleared her throat. "Sorry."

"Something wrong?" he asked. "You sound distracted. Bad day?"

Brittany sighed. "Actually I was on my way to Wade's office to discuss a claim."

"Well, I won't keep you long. I thought I'd see if you wanted to have dinner tonight."

Brittany drummed her long, highly polished nails on the desk while she thought. "I'll take a rain check if you don't mind. I'm not sure I'll be in town this evening."

When she didn't elaborate, Howard said, "All right. But the day you get back, call me. We need to talk."

"I know," Brittany responded, a sinking feeling in the pit of her stomach.

He no longer bothered to hide his frustration or his wanning patience. She heard them in his voice. She guessed it was time to have that talk, to sever their relationship, actually. She hated to, but it wasn't fair to him. He deserved more than the crumbs of her life she threw him.

"Later, then."

"Later," Brittany said lightly, and placed the dead receiver into its cradle.

She didn't know how long she'd sat there, her thoughts in chaos, before she heard a sharp, brief tap on her door.

"Come in," she said, and watched as Wade Bryant strode through the door.

He was short and thick and wore thick glasses that made his eyes look abnormally large. He had a compulsion for neatness, especially when it came to his spectacles. They were never smudged; he made polishing them a ritual. His compulsiveness, among other things, made Brittany nervous. It was all she could do to tolerate him.

"Perfect timing," she remarked as he plopped down in the chair in front of her desk. "I was just on my way to see you."

"Oh."

She heard the wary surprise in his voice and almost smiled. It was no secret that she and Wade didn't work well together. But it wasn't because she hadn't tried. He resented her for who she was and didn't try to hide it.

Unfortunately, Walter had only praise for him. He touted Wade's knowledge of the insurance business and had complete confidence in him. Brittany wasn't so gung ho. She worked with him every day, saw a side of Wade her daddy didn't see. Wade was dogmatic and refused to gamble on anything. Most of the time it took a surgical procedure to get him to try a new idea. But she kept on trying. Today would be no exception.

"I've been looking through that logger's file," Brittany said, bridging the lengthy silence.

"The one outside of Lufkin?"

"Right. His name is Matthew Diamond."

"Found something interesting, I take it?"

"Very."

Wade flicked a tiny piece of white lint off his dark suit trousers, then looked at her directly. "Good. We'll discuss it at the meeting I've called at seven in the morning."

"I hope I won't be here."

Wade raised an eyebrow. "And just where will you be?"

"In Lufkin. Or rather, the outskirts, I should say."

"I don't think so."

Brittany smiled thinly. "And why not?"

Wade stood abruptly. "Because it's not your case. I've decided to let Hamilton handle it, though I'm sure he'll be interested in hearing your assessment."

Brittany stood, as well. Her green eyes flashed. "Hamilton already has more cases than he can handle. I want this one."

"No way," Wade said flatly, and leaned over, planting both hands in the middle of the file.

Brittany swallowed the sharp retort that came to mind and stepped back. He smelled as though he'd soaked himself in Brut. But that wasn't why she avoided him. She feared she'd slap his smug face.

If she lost her temper, she would play into Wade's hands. That was what he wanted, what he expected her to do. He tested her relentlessly, alert to something, anything, that would make her look bad in Walter's eyes. But he was cagey about it; his claws were covered in syrup.

She never rose to the occasion, though, much to his chagrin. She did the work assigned to her and did it so well he couldn't find fault.

But this particular case was different. She wanted it and was prepared to fight for it. Not only was it a challenge, but it was a chance to prove her worth to the company and to her daddy.

"I'm perfectly capable of handling this case, Wade."

"I don't think so." His voice turned cold. "Diamond is obviously playing the company for a fool, and I want to get him."

"Me, too."

"For heaven's sake, tromping through the woods is the last place you need to be."

"That's ridiculous," Brittany countered hotly. "Anyway, tromping through the woods, as you so aptly phrased it, is not what this is about. There's more to it than that."

He smiled in a superior way. "I've made up my mind. Nothing you say will change it."

"We'll see about that." Brittany's quietly spoken words had the same effect as if she'd slapped him.

Wade's head snapped back, and his eyes narrowed behind his glasses. "Exactly what are you saying?"

"I'm saying that I've done my best to do things your way. I've taken your veiled insults, your contemptuous looks and your condemnation of my work. But no longer. I want this case, and if I have to, I'll go over your head."

Wade's upper lip developed an odd tic. "And what makes you think your daddy will side with you?"

"Are you prepared to take the chance?"

Color washed Wade's face; he appeared to be having an attack of high blood pressure. "All right," he snapped. "Take it, but you damn well better come back with the ammunition to cancel Diamond or—"

"Or what?"

He stared at her for a long moment. His Adam's apple slid up and down as if he wanted to say something but couldn't. Then he pivoted on the heels of his polished shoes and walked toward the door.

He reached for the knob, only to have the door suddenly open. Walter Fleming stood on the threshold.

Wade inclined his head and strode past him.

Fleming turned to Brittany, a perplexed frown on his face. "What was that all about?"

"Hello, Daddy," Brittany said with a warm smile. "Nothing, really."

"You sure about that? Wade looked ready to explode."

"Well, we did have a slight disagreement," Brittany admitted reluctantly.

Walter crossed to the coffee bar in the far corner of the room and helped himself to a generous cup of coffee. Brittany examined him from under a screen of thick lashes, thinking how different she and her daddy were in both looks and temperament.

He was a bland-looking man in his early sixties. A slightly bald head, long, lean face, brown eyes and a pale complexion best described him. Both his height and weight were average.

There was nothing average about his mind, however, or his energy level. Both were razor sharp and always active. And when he wanted to, he could turn on the charm. It was that charm, combined with his intelligence, that had made him into the rich and respected businessman he was today.

While Brittany favored her mother in looks, she had inherited her daddy's keen mind—and the charm. Like him, she was not above using it to get what she wanted.

"Mm, this coffee's good. First time I've stopped all day." He set the cup down. "So what were you and Wade discussing?"

"The Diamond case. Are you familiar with it?"

"Vaguely. Wade said he'd turn it over to Hamilton."

"I told him I wanted it."

Walter's eyebrows shot up. "Think you can handle it?"

"Yes, I do," Brittany said, turning away.

"From the side, you look just like your mother." Walter's tone was brusque.

Brittany broke into a smile. "I'll take that as a compliment," she said softly.

"You should—she was lovely."

A poignant silence followed his unexpected admission—the only sound the chiming of the grandfather clock on the wall.

There had been many women in his life since his wife's death, but he had never remarried. Many times Brittany wished he had, more for her sake than for his.

"So you're going to go after this Diamond fellow, huh?"

"If he's trying to cheat us, I'll get him."

Walter stared at her for an intense minute, as if he saw her for the first time. "That's my girl, a chip off the old block. Go to it."

A glow surrounded Brittany's heart. "Thanks, Daddy, I will."

When she walked out of the office a short time later, briefcase in hand, she couldn't seem to stop smiling.

Three

"**D**amn!"

Sam whined and thumped his tail in response to Matt's muttered curse.

Matt ignored Sam and cursed again. Matt's shoulders felt as though they had a sack of steel across them. So did his back and legs.

The mutt thumped his tail that much longer, as if he resented Matt ignoring him.

"Sam, what was I thinking about when I decided to go into the logging business? I must've been outa my mind."

But, setbacks aside, he loved what he did, loved being in the woods, being his own boss. And while things were about as grim as they could be, he clung to the hope that his luck was about to change.

That attitude was becoming increasingly hard to hang on to, especially after he'd put in two hours of hard labor. He'd fixed a gas leak in his only mobile loader, a leak that threatened to shut him down completely if he couldn't repair it.

Matt straightened, then grimaced. God, he was tired. Before coming to the work shed, he'd already put in hard hours in the woods. He glanced at his watch and saw that it was five o'clock. He'd been on the job since dawn, along with Elmer. They had gotten as much done as possible with only one loader and skidder.

His day hadn't stopped there. When he'd gotten home, he'd headed to the workshop and had been there ever since. He bent over the hood once again and unscrewed another bolt. His thoughts dwelled on the insurance company. They were taking their own sweet time in settling. But then, what else was new? He hated insurance companies, hated them with a passion. Unfortunately, though, they were a necessary evil, especially in his line of work.

He just wished they would get a move on. At this rate, he'd be out of business before they arrived. Not only was he worried about his equipment payments, which were going to be late, if not skipped entirely this month, but he was worried about his employees, as well. They depended on him for a living. They had families to feed, and he felt lower than a snake's belly when he couldn't work them.

Sweat trickled into Matt's eyes and blurred them. He paused and wiped the back of his hand across his forehead. It was then he heard the car. At first he thought it was Elmer returning to help him, although he'd told him not to. Elmer had been sick to his stomach when they'd left the woods, and Matt had ordered him to go home and go to bed.

Sam heard the sound, too. His ears stood straight up.

"Looks like we got company, boy."

Although Matt lifted his head from under the hood of the truck, he didn't move out of the shadow into the direct light. He watched as the vehicle wound its way up the long drive. His visitor was behind the wheel of a late model Chrysler LeBaron, convertible no less, though the top was not down.

He knew without being told that the dress-for-success adjuster had arrived. Only politicians, doctors and insurance executives drove cars like that, he thought, a sudden bad taste developing in his mouth.

Sam stood beside him and growled.

"Well, I'll be damned, Sam, it's a woman."

She hadn't seen him yet, which was definitely to his advantage. He'd been expecting an adjuster, all right, but not a woman. Matt placed his hand on Sam's head. The dog instantly stopped growling and stood still.

The woman stopped the car between the house and the shed and got out. Matt sucked in his breath. She was beautiful; even from where he was he could see that. Her short, curly hair shone like a bronze chrysanthemum. Not only that, but she possessed a body that had more curves than a road map, although they were somewhat tempered by her business suit.

Once she was out of the car, she took a few steps. He liked the way she walked; her hips swayed—perfection in motion. Realizing the track his thoughts had taken, he cursed silently. But still he watched as she shielded her eyes with a long-fingered hand and gazed around.

Damn! he thought, thrusting his head under the hood. Why did the company send a woman? As badly as he needed to settle the claim, and they sent a woman who probably knew less about the logging business than he did about women's cosmetics.

Brittany blinked against the harsh sunlight. Even though the calender said May, the weather felt more like summer than spring. Beads of perspiration gathered under the arms of her silk blouse, tempting her to pull off her jacket. No. She wanted to appear as businesslike as possible when she confronted Matthew Diamond.

Being a woman put her at a disadvantage. This part of East Texas was known as redneck country, which meant they weren't tolerant of much, especially female strangers.

Brittany had arrived later than she'd intended. She had meant to leave Tyler earlier, only it hadn't worked out. She'd had another pressing claim she couldn't ignore. Still, she had forced herself to stay within the speed limit and enjoy the scenic countryside. Highway 69 between Tyler and Lufkin was beautiful this time of year. A blaze of colorful wildflowers dotted the highway while tall oaks and pines lined the horizon.

But now Brittany's mind was definitely not on the sights and sounds around her. It was focused on her job. Crazy as it seemed, this was the claim that could make or break her. Her knowledge and credibility were on the line.

Last night at home she had reviewed the case well into the night. She had also crammed her head full of logging terms and information, determined to be in charge. Once again, those terms flashed before her eyes, and she reviewed them.

Set is the working area around a pile of logs.

Chain saw cuts the fallen trees into lengths.

Skidder goes after the trees.

Grapple on back of skidder grabs logs and drags to set.

Loader loads them and takes them to truck.

She'd been tempted to delay this visit. She'd needed more time to prepare. But she had ignored the urge to check into a motel room before she searched for the Diamond place, afraid if she waited till morning, Matthew Diamond would be in the woods. This way she could at least meet her client and size up the situation.

Despite her Ray Bans, Brittany found the sunlight offensive. She had to admit it was lovely here, though much too secluded for her taste. Give her the city anytime. Country living was not for her.

Matt Diamond's part-brick, part-frame house wasn't bad, either. A bit on the small side, but neat and trim just the same. But it wasn't his house she had to worry about; it was his equipment.

Should she knock on the door? It was so quiet and silent she began to doubt anyone was home. She took a hesitant step toward the front door, and at the same time her gaze wandered off. She saw the work shed nestled among a cluster of spindly oaks. She paused, then thought, why not? If he wasn't there, no harm done.

The truck's raised hood was the first thing she saw. The dog was the second. The animal glared at her, then growled.

"Good doggie," Brittany cajoled, just as something moved behind the hood. "Mr. Diamond?"

Brittany didn't know what she expected Matthew Diamond to look like, hadn't even thought about it. But the man that stepped out from behind the truck was nothing like she would have envisioned, not in a million years.

"Yeah?"

"I'm . . . I'm Brittany Fleming from—"

"The insurance agency," he finished for her, his voice as cold as an Arctic winter. He slammed down the hood of the truck and stepped into full view. "And Daddy's little girl, to boot—right?"

A gasp rippled through Brittany as her astonished gaze traveled over a deeply tanned face with lean features. A nose that had been broken, a thin-lipped mouth and a strong chin would not have struck her as sexy, but on him they were.

His jawline was dark. He needed a shave, although she guessed he had shaved that morning. His hair, wet with sweat, should have looked shaggy because it was too long. But it didn't. He should have looked indecent in a pair of faded, low-riding jeans. But he didn't. Instead he looked like a savage with muscled shoulders and biceps that were bathed in sweat and grease.

She had the most ludicrous urge to reach out and wipe one greasy mark off his chest...

"So am I right?" he asked, and it took a minute before she realized what he was talking about. A wave of horror washed over her. Somehow, she had lost control of her thoughts. She struggled to answer him before he caught on that something was wrong.

But he had noticed. His appraisal of her spoke volumes.

"It makes no difference who I am," she said in a frigid tone. "But since you asked, I am the boss's daughter."

"Okay, so where's the check?"

"I don't have it."

"Hell," he muttered.

If the smart-aleck hostility that dropped off him like icicles wasn't enough to unlock her frozen limbs, then the anger behind that soft, spoken word should have been. Neither did. She continued to stand there subject to the same scrutiny she had given him.

His deep-set blue eyes were like hot knives, dissecting her. Her body felt them like blows.

She tried to look away. She *wanted* to look away. Her mouth was dry. Her heart beat much too fast. But she couldn't make a move.

Their gazes remained locked. The moment was electric. The look that bound them had nothing to do with the sparse words they had just exchanged. In fact the words were totally forgotten. There was such a searing intimacy in that exchange that Brittany's limbs felt scorched. It was all she could do to keep her control from disintegrating.

And then it was over as quickly as it had begun. Matt's face went blank and his lids lowered, leaving her with the uncanny suspicion that she had imagined the whole thing.

"Now where were we?" he drawled, his eyes on her face, disturbingly intent. "Ah, yes, I remember. I asked if you had my check."

Struggling to keep her defensive shell intact, Brittany cleared her throat and in her most businesslike tone said, "And I said no."

"Why not?"

"Look, Mr. Diamond, you know why not."

"No, suppose you tell me."

She wouldn't let him fluster her again. She wouldn't. "You know very well I have to investigate the legitimacy of your claims."

"Insurance companies are all alike." His voice was laced with bitterness. "They're nothing but a bunch of thieves. They take your money, then when they have to cough up in return, no dice. So why don't you make it easy on both of us and just write me a check?"

Brittany bit back a retort. If she stooped to his level, entered into a verbal match with him, she'd never get her work accomplished. Right now that was utmost in her mind. She must take care of business and get out of there.

"We both know that's not going to happen. I may as well tell you up front, the company is taking a dim view of your claims."

Matt came toward her. He moved like a wild animal—fluidly, silently. "I don't give a tinker's dam what view they take as long as they fork over the money."

Brittany backed up, but not before their eyes met again, this time as two enemies sizing up each other. If the blatant sexual appreciation had been there a moment ago, there was no sign of it now.

"Well, then, you let me do my job and we'll see. I need to see the damaged equipment, ask questions."

"Not today, lady. It's too late. I'm bone tired and I'm calling it a day."

Twin flags of color stained her cheeks. "Are you always this rude and uncooperative?"

Matt crossed his arms and smiled with no warmth. "I guess you'll just have to find that out for yourself, won't you?"

"I'll be back tomorrow, Mr. Diamond," she snapped. "Be ready to answer my questions. That is, if you want any money."

This time, he flushed.

Good, Brittany thought. It was about time she ruffled his calm. Money would do it every time.

"I'll be in the woods till noon." At best, his tone was surly.

"I'll see you after lunch, then." With that she turned and made her way to her car. She had the door open and was about to get in when she saw him lean against the hood.

"What is it now?"

"Your rear tire is low."

Brittany's eyes followed his. "Terrific."

"Want me to change it?"

"No, thank you," she said waspishly. "I'll take care of it when I get back to...civilization."

His lips curved in a small, secret smile. "Suit yourself."

"I intend to, Mr. Diamond," Brittany said, slamming the car door. "I intend to."

She was halfway down the drive before she looked in the rearview mirror. He hadn't moved. He was watching her with that smart-aleck grin well in place.

Damn him.

Four

Two beers hadn't helped Matt's disposition one iota. Nor had a cold shower. He was in a lousy mood. It didn't take a rocket scientist to see the handwriting on the wall. Trouble was brewing—in the name of Brittany Fleming.

But it sure as hell was wrapped in a gorgeous package. Up close, she'd looked even better than she had at a distance. He was sure her face must be a photographer's dream—high cheekbones, full sensuous mouth and milk-white skin. And those wide-spaced, sharp green eyes flashed as sharply as her tongue.

What had he done to deserve the likes of her? The last thing he needed was a high-and-mighty female who thought she was better than most folks, nosing around and questioning his actions and his integrity.

Maybe she wouldn't come back tomorrow.

"Think that's possible, Sam? Think she'll turn tail and run?"

Sam stared at him with soleful eyes as Matt took another swig of beer.

"Naw, you're right, she won't. Hell would freeze over before that broad would back down."

He'd seen the contempt in her eyes, and that was what made him the maddest. But he'd also seen the way she'd looked at him, like she could eat him with a spoon. Of course, she would have denied that—if he'd called her hand on it, that is. People like *her* didn't desire someone like *him*. No, sir. It was beneath their dignity. But he hadn't been mistaken; for a moment, something had sizzled between them.

She wasn't the first female to appreciate his body. He'd seen that look before, many times, and he'd made the most of it. Hell, just because he lived alone didn't mean he had to. There had been a lot of women in and out of his life, but none had ever gotten past the shield around his heart. He never allowed that.

He'd been in love once. But the desire to marry had died with her. He'd met Wendy Sheffield three days after he'd arrived in Saudi Arabia, in a grocery store, of all places. She'd been a teacher in an American school. In her quiet, sweet, unassuming way, she had managed to crack that shield, and he had thought at last he'd found a woman who understood him. He had wanted to share his life with her.

Only she'd gotten killed in an automobile accident six months after he'd asked her to marry him.

Since then, he'd lost count of the women who had shared his bed. Sure, he was more careful now. But that was the only thing that had changed. Commitment to one woman was out of the question, especially one like Brittany Fleming.

Yet he couldn't help but wonder what it would be like to take this particular product of high-class society into a hotel room, stretch her across a bed and make love to her until they were both exhausted. He felt sure that it would be an experience he'd never forget.

"Dream on, Diamond." He downed the last of his beer in one swallow.

What he needed was to put that woman out of his mind, get cleaned up and eat something. Brittany Fleming had ruined his day; he refused to let her ruin his evening, as well.

Although the shower felt good, he didn't linger. His stomach growled from lack of food. He slipped into a pair of jeans and ambled into the kitchen, only to groan when he opened the refrigerator. Empty, except for beer.

"Great."

Well, he guessed Annie's Padlock Café would get his business again. In fact, if it weren't for Annie's he'd starve to death. It might be a dive but it was the best place in town to eat. He ought to know; he ate there seven days a week. Maybe one of the these days he'd get around to going to the grocery store.

A few minutes later, Matt turned onto the farm road that would eventually take him onto the highway. He saw her then. Actually, he saw her snazzy automobile first. The tire was as flat as flat could be.

She sat behind the wheel, and he guessed she had just about reached the boiling point by now, although it had been only an hour since she'd left. Her arrogant statement, "I'll take care of it when I get back to...civilization," still echoed in the piney woods.

He threw back his head and laughed.

A good deal of that laughter shined in his eyes as he pulled his Ford Ranger pickup behind her car and got out. He saw her look at him out of the corner of her eyes, though she kept her face pointed straight ahead.

"Well, well...what have we here?"

As if his mocking tone was more than she could take, Brittany twisted her head and said, "Don't you dare say it!"

"Say what?" He grinned and leaned against her car. "Say that I told you so?"

She lifted her chin slightly. "Go ahead, have your fun. But the last laugh will be on me. You'll see."

He crossed his arms over his chest and stared at her. "Oh, and just how do you figure that? Seems to me, I can fix your flat or choose to let you sit here and fume."

Brittany looked alarmed. "You wouldn't. It'll...it'll soon be dark," she added on a plaintive note.

"Well?"

"Well, what?" she asked, crossing her legs.

Matt didn't respond right off. He couldn't. He was too busy tracking a tiny run in one of her nylon hose, only to have it disappear at the hemline of her skirt.

Where did it end? At the top of her thigh? His imagination went wild.

"Well, what?" she repeated in an irritated voice.

Matt jerked his eyes off her, off *it*, then cursed himself for such foolishness. Another moment lapsed before he cleared his throat and said, "You know what." He spoke more roughly than he intended.

"No, I don't." Her muscles seemed to tighten under his tone. "Stop playing games."

"Then say the magic word."

"And just what is that?"

A display of innocence widened his eyes. "If you don't know, then I guess I'll be on my way. I was about to grab a bite to eat. Too bad you can't join me."

"Cute," she said sarcastically.

He waved a hand. "If that's your final word, I'll be on my way."

"Don't you dare walk away from me!"

He kept on walking.

"All right!"

He slowly turned and waited.

Brittany balled her fingers into fists, while her lower lip stuck out like a sulky child's. "*Please*, would you change my tire?"

"Why, ma'am," he said mockingly, "I thought you'd never ask."

"Go to hell."

His eyes instantly locked with hers. He was not amused. "I'd be careful what I wished for, if I were you. What goes around comes around."

* * *

Brittany didn't know how long she'd been pacing the carpet in her stark motel room.

When Matt had finished changing the tire, she had driven to a filling station and left the flat one, then found a motel and checked in. She had lain across the bed, but figured sleep would be a long time in coming simply because she was so frustrated at the way her day had turned out. She kept thinking about all those terms she'd memorized, how she'd planned to show off her knowledge, and her anger mounted.

Nevertheless, she'd fallen asleep and hadn't awakened until the sun peeped through the flimsy curtains. She'd jumped out of bed, appalled that she'd actually slept in her clothes.

As she continued her pacing, Brittany eyed the bag she'd slung across the bed and hadn't bothered to open. She felt grimy and wanted a shower desperately. But she was too pumped up mentally and physically to do anything constructive.

She would go home. It was that simple. She wouldn't waste another second of valuable time on that obstinate, opinionated, hardheaded redneck.

Let someone else from the office take him on. She didn't have to put up with his smart mouth or his seething looks. Why, the way his eyes had scaled her body, you'd think he hadn't had a woman in lord knows how long. And not for one second did she take his perusal of her as a compliment.

Then why was her pulse racing? Okay, so she was intrigued as well as angry. She'd concede that. After all, she'd never met a man quite like him. The earthy type was nonexistent in her world. The men she'd dated as a rule wore three-piece suits, *not* tight-fitting jeans, boots and hat. And they certainly wore shirts, for heaven's sake!

Still, that aspect was what had unnerved her, what kept her pulse racing and her heart beating rapidly. He had a great body; as a sexual entity, he was dynamite. But that was as far as it went. Matthew Diamond did not interest her, not really. And what's more, she didn't have to take his snide comments or put up with his hot eyes raking her.

"So stop your bitching, pick up your bags and go home." Speaking aloud had a sudden and profoundly calming effect on Brittany. She stopped, took a deep breath and eased down on the side of the bed, completely ignoring the squeaking springs.

She couldn't go home. To do so would be admitting defeat, and she wasn't about to do that. She had something to prove to her daddy, and she was going to do it. Nothing could undermine that. She would face her adversary today, work around his verbal abuse and do the job she had been sent to do. And he'd cooperate or she'd personally see that he wouldn't get one dime of insurance money.

Without wasting another second, she snatched her bag and marched into the bathroom. Thirty minutes later she was ready to go.

No man was going to defeat her, certainly not Matthew Diamond. Before she was through with him, he'd be the one begging.

The thought was so delicious, she smiled.

Five

___

She found him in the workshop, standing over a huge chain saw as if pondering its fate. Brittany knew he'd heard her car, yet he acted as if he hadn't.

His hair was still damp from the shower, she noticed. He obviously hadn't been back from the woods long. He wore faded jeans and an equally faded blue T-shirt chopped off at the waist, which made him look rougher, tougher and sexier. He was the quintessential bad boy, the kind mothers see in their nightmares and girls see in their dreams.

But she was no girl. Yet she was stricken with the same malady. What was her excuse? Brittany fought against the tremors that suddenly weakened her all over and kept her from moving. This man was a menace—and she'd best remember that.

"Mr. Diamond."

Matt lifted his head and stared at her through hostile eyes, their coldness a shock to her already scattered senses. She refused to let him browbeat her, or for that matter know that he had upset her at all.

Brittany lifted her chin a notch. "I take it you didn't expect to see me."

"As a matter of fact, I didn't," he said flatly.

"I told you I'd be here, and I meant it."

Matt turned his back on the chain saw, then sauntered out of the shadow of the trees and into the light. Again Brittany was caught short by the picture he presented. The wind stroked his damp hair and loosened the near-blond strands. And what the sun did for his tan couldn't be put into words.

"Well, I can't say I'm not surprised—because I am." A muscle ticked in his right jaw, and his tone mocked her. "I thought for sure you'd be snug in your own bed in Tyler by now."

He stopped within touching distance of her. Brittany was forced to look up and meet the rock hardness of his gaze, which bore into her as if he searched for something.

The air seemed to thicken, brought on by a heightened tension that flared between them. What was he thinking? Brittany wondered, holding her breath.

The afternoon breeze suddenly whipped a lock of hair across her cheek. She brushed it back, breaking eye contact with him in the process.

He moved restlessly, then jammed his hands into his pockets. "Since you're here, let's get down to business. If you know your business, that is."

"Make no mistake. *I* know what I'm doing." Her tone was acidic. "Correct me if I'm wrong, but it's your business that's in trouble." She knew she was being childish and argumentative, but there was something about this man that brought out the worst in her.

Matt's anger and impatience were obvious, but when he spoke, his words were calm and without malice. "Look, let's call a truce, okay? All I want is my money."

"Well, unless you cooperate to the fullest, you won't get your money, Mr. Diamond. And whether you like it or not, you're stuck with the company. And me."

He acted as if he wanted to say something else, but he didn't. Instead he started walking. Brittany matched him stride for stride.

"Before we look at the damaged equipment," she said, "I need some general information."

"Fire away."

At a wing of the covered shed, Brittany popped the snap of her shoulder bag and pulled out a notebook with pen attached.

Matt leaned against the building, as if he didn't have a care in the world. She knew better; the sheen of sweat on his upper lip gave lie to that pose. Inside he was coiled tight and ready to spring. Not only was this man a menace, but he was dangerous, as well. Maybe that was where the challenge lay. She enjoyed flirting with danger, always had and always would.

"I need your employees' social security numbers and driver's licenses," she finally said.

"Do you mind if I ask why?"

Brittany searched for the sarcasm that was hidden in that question, but she couldn't quite pin it down.

"The company needs to run a criminal check on them."

"What about me?" He smirked. "Do they need one on me, too?"

"Yes." She flushed in spite of her efforts not to do so. Damn her fair skin.

"Oh, that's rich. Surely you don't think—"

Brittany shook her head, stopping him. "The company's not picking on you."

"What about you, Ms. Fleming? Are *you* picking on me?"

She knew she should ignore him, as he was deliberately goading her. But she couldn't. Matt Diamond was not the type you ignored.

"No," she said, with an exasperated lift of her shoulders, an action that pulled the material of her gold silk blouse tightly across her breasts, momentarily accenting their fullness. It was an unconscious gesture on her part, something that would have gone unnoticed had it not been for him. Matt's eyes lowered to that exact spot and stayed there.

Sparks exploded inside her just as she saw the confused anger in his eyes. Obviously he was disturbed as much as she was. What was happening here?

He ripped his gaze away, and the world suddenly righted itself.

Brittany arranged a smile on her face and forced a calmness into her voice. "What I'm doing is standard operating procedure."

"I have several steady employees."

She clicked her pen and prepared to write. "And they are?"

"Right now, I'm only working Elmer Cayhill and Billy Frost. My run of bad luck forced me to let the others go."

Using a nearby tree as their base, a blue jay and a squirrel played tag. Brittany watched them for a moment, thinking how uncomplicated their lives were. Then she shook herself mentally and said, "I suppose you have the information I need on them in your office."

"Right."

"I...I can get that later," she said, swallowing hard, conscious again of his unsettling closeness. He smelled like the woods, strong but fresh. She stepped back.

His expression hardened, but he didn't say anything.

Brittany looked down quickly and consulted another page in her notebook, then looked up. "Our records show you with seven pieces of heavy equipment."

He nodded.

"Out of the seven you've filed claims on four."

"They are legit claims, Ms. Fleming."

She prayed for patience. "Regardless, they have to be checked out, especially since they happened within an eight-month period."

"Trust me, it happens all the time." His glance was cool and impersonal.

"I don't think so."

"Oh, is that right? Since when did you become an expert?" His voice was heavy with ridicule.

"I don't claim to be an expert," she lashed back, "but it seems to me that it's a bit odd that so much has gone wrong so quickly."

"Well, I hate to burst your bubble, but in this business anything can happen at any time."

"You're not the only logger we insure, and to date no one has filed this many claims this close together."

"I don't like what you're insinuating."

Brittany's coral-glazed lips tightened. "I'm not insinuating anything. I'm merely gathering the facts."

He snorted. "Yeah."

A short, hostile silence followed. Brittany broke it first. "Might I remind you that we've already paid off on the first burned skidder."

"Are you saying I should pin a medal on you for doing your job?"

"You're impossible." She felt her voice slide out of control.

"So I've been told." He seemed to rally unaffected by her fit of temper. "By the way," he drawled, "why didn't the adjustor that was here before come back?"

"He's on another case."

"Really?"

"Yes, really," Brittany lied.

He looked at her for a long moment, then said in a bored tone, "What else do you want to know?"

Brittany released her pent-up breath. She hated telling a little white lie, but she wasn't about to tell him she had fought for this case. If she had known then what she knew now, would she have taken it? No, not if she were in her right mind.

"I need to see the skidder that caught on fire and the loader that was vandalized."

"Follow me."

Silence accompanied them to the first heavy piece of equipment. Brittany eyed it carefully. "This is the loader." It was a statement rather than a question.

Before they had left the shed, Matt had grabbed a battered Stetson off a nail on the wall and slapped it on. Now he tipped it back and eyed her carefully, his lips quirked in a half smile. "Yeah, that's a loader."

She didn't try to hide her anger. "Don't you dare patronize me! I know what I'm doing," she added in a more conciliatory tone. If she ever wanted to get this chore over with, she had to stop letting him needle her. It was as simple and as complicated as that.

He merely shrugged, then said, "I'm listening."

"Where was the skidder?"

"Here, under the shed."

"Where did the fire start?"

"In the engine room."

"What caused it? Did a battery cable short out or was it perhaps from neglect?"

"You just don't know when to give it a rest, do you?"

"It's a valid question, and you know it."

"I see that the engines are washed and cleaned as often as needed. So you can forget the neglect angle."

"Just how often is that?" Brittany pressed.

"Sometimes every other day." His voice cracked like the sound of a lash on raw flesh.

She didn't so much as flinch. "What about the fire extinguisher? Why wasn't it used to put the fire out?"

"Because the skidder caught on fire during the night, that's why."

Brittany didn't respond. She didn't want to give him that satisfaction. Instead, she wrote down his explanation. When she finished, she looked at him, but avoided his gaze. She felt it, though, and it deepened her agitation. "Let's see the loader that was vandalized."

"It's over there." Matt motioned with his hand, then waited for her to go ahead of him.

She'd taken a few steps when she turned to say something to him, only to nearly bump into his chest.

"Oh," she said a trifle breathlessly.

A hand shot out to steady her. He glanced down. His eyes found and lingered a fraction of a second on her lips. But it was long enough to ignite her imagination as to how it would feel to have his mouth on hers.

Was she crazy? The last thing she wanted to do was get sexually involved with this man. She was stunned that such a thought could cross her mind, no matter how fleetingly.

Her face burning, she stepped away and murmured, "Sorry."

"No harm done," Matt said, in such an odd voice that it drew her eyes to his. His face gave nothing away. But there was something in his eyes, something she couldn't identify. Naked desire?

Brittany licked her dry lips. "Tell me about the loader."

They stood beside it.

"There's not a lot to tell. It was parked in the woods. The next morning the damn thing had been worked over."

"How?"

Matt's face was grim. "Tires were flat, and as you can see, they beat the hell out of the instrument panel."

"Anything else?" Brittany asked, her pen busy.

"Yeah. The s.o.b.s put sand in the fuel system."

"Kids?"

Exasperation changed his expression. "Don't know. It could've been. But it could also have been other loggers."

Brittany was taken aback. "Other loggers? Why on earth—"

"Simple. This can be a cutthroat business, and some around these parts are jealous if you're success-ful and they aren't."

"Any other possibilities?"

"Hunters. They're notorious for trying to run log-gers off property on or close to where they hunt."

Brittany frowned.

"Not a pretty picture, is it?"

"No, it's not."

They were silent for a moment. The warm after-noon sun beat down on them. Brittany placed the back of her hand against her lips to keep from yawning.

He saw the gesture and smiled.

She stared at him, aghast.

"What's wrong?" he asked sharply.

Brittany held his gaze, though clearly flustered. "It's nothing, actually. It's just that you smiled, really smiled."

He blinked.

"For a second there, you were almost human," she said.

He turned away, as if the sudden warmth in her eyes was too disturbing. "I'll bear that in mind."

"About the truck," Brittany asked, realizing how close she had come to making a fool of herself. Who cared if he ever smiled or not? "I need to know—"

"It'll have to wait," he said abruptly, looking beyond her shoulder.

"Why?"

"Company."

Brittany swung around. A young man who looked to be in his early twenties was beside the work shed. He walked toward them. He had longish, unkept brown hair and sullen features.

"Who's he?" Brittany asked, frowning.

"Billy Frost, one of my hands."

"Somehow I can't see him working for you."

"Oh?"

She hesitated. "I guess what I mean to say is that he seems a little... Oh, forget it. I don't know what I meant."

"You're right. Under ordinary circumstances, he couldn't work for me, but since the accident—" Matt broke off suddenly and clamped his jaws together.

"What accident?"

"Never mind," he said tersely. "It doesn't concern you."

Brittany bit back a retort and asked instead, "Shall I leave you two alone?"

"I'm sure he's come to borrow money."

"Borrow money?"

"That's right. My hands depend on me to work them, and when I can't, they're in deep trouble."

"I see."

"I doubt that," Matt responded flatly. "I'd be willing to bet you've never wanted for anything in your life."

Brittany opened her mouth to retaliate when he waved a hand and said, "Save it."

He turned his back on her and started toward the Frost boy.

"I'll leave, but I'll be back tomorrow," Brittany said.

He paused slightly, then kept on walking.

Six

"When do you think we'll be back in full operation?"

Matt wiped the grease off his hands, tossed the rag aside, then faced Elmer. "I wish I knew. In two weeks my equipment note is due, and I flat can't make it."

"It's a damn shame this had to happen now," Elmer said. "With the mill wanting as much timber as we can haul, we'd be in the catbird seat."

"Tell me," Matt responded.

They had come from the woods, tended to the equipment and were about to go to their respective homes to get a shower. They had quit early, after moving the equipment to a new location where they would start afresh the following morning.

Matt sighed inwardly, glanced at his watch and noticed that the time was nearly two o'clock.

Elmer scratched his whiskery face. "I saw a couple of the men yesterday in town. They're hurtin' real bad." Hating to add to Matt's burden, he spoke in reluctant tones.

"I know, Elmer. No work, no pay. I made that clear when I hired them."

"Hey, I'm not faulting you. It's just that none of the other low-life contractors will hire them because they know the minute you get back in full operation, the men will hightail it back to you."

Matt's brow drew together in a heavy frown. "It's a mess, all right." He paused. "Billy came by yesterday and asked for money."

"Did you let him have it?"

"A few dollars, that's all."

"That kid bothers me. He's nothing like his brother. You sure he's not adopted? Or maybe his mother dropped him on his head when he was born, 'cause he's sure a few bricks shy of a load."

Matt grinned and slapped Elmer on the shoulder. "Very eloquently put, my friend. He gets on my nerves, too, if that's any consolation."

"Very little."

"You tell the fellows next time you see 'em that if they get in a real jam, look me up." Matt's features were again brooding and uncertain.

"Will do."

The men were quiet for a moment. Then Elmer said, "You can tell me to mind my own business if you've a mind to, but—"

Matt made a gesture. "You know better than that."

"Well, I know the insurance adjuster's here. So how soon do you think you'll be getting your money?"

"That's a damn good question. She's giving me trouble."

"She? Did you say *she?*"

"That was my reaction, too."

Elmer shook his head. "What's this world coming to? Sending a woman..."

"I know. I don't like it, either, but I have no choice but to deal with her." Matt looked at his watch again. "She's due any minute."

This time it was Elmer who slapped Matt on the back. "Well, in that case, I'm outa here. Good luck, boy. That's all I have to say."

"Thanks," Matt said drolly.

Elmer ambled in the direction of his truck, mumbling out loud, "A woman..."

Matt's thoughts were the same, maybe worse, when six o'clock rolled around and Brittany hadn't arrived.

There were a million things he could have done around the place, paperwork for one, but instead he'd showered and dressed. Brittany's pending arrival had consumed his thoughts and energy.

And the longer he waited, the angrier he became.

Where the hell was she? He didn't even know where she was staying. He could find out, of course, and easily enough, only he hadn't thought it was necessary. Till now.

He felt as if the walls were closing in on him. He grabbed his hat and stomped to the door. There, he turned and whistled.

The hound thundered eagerly down the hall. His tongue hung out and his tail wagged.

"Come on, boy, let's go."

Sam nuzzled his hand.

He'd give her ten more minutes, Matt told himself, glancing at his watch for the umpteenth time. To hell with her. He was hungry; he was going to the Padlock and have himself a piece of beef as big as his hand.

He gave a damn only because the longer she took to make the claim, the longer it would take to get his money. Or at least this was what he told himself.

He knew better, though. Brittany was under his skin. She was an annoyance—a ravishing, pampered, luscious annoyance. An annoyance he didn't want to stop.

Crazy thoughts like that scared him, made him edgy. Without exception, he'd made a point to avoid the Brittanys of the world. That had been easy because they'd never really interested him—too cool, too unapproachable. He didn't want a woman he would have to thaw first.

Brittany didn't fool him. He knew her kind. She thought she was better than the average person. But her upper-crust snobbery didn't impress him. He saw her for what she was. Still, he wanted her—gut deep, he wanted her. But thank God that gnawing in his gut was only temporary. "Out of sight, out of mind" was written for him. She was just a passing fancy, and once she was gone, he'd settle down.

In the meantime, where did that leave him? Mad, for one thing. And for another, wanting.

Sam whined.

Matt grimaced. "I agree, boy. Time's up."

Several seconds later, his pickup was lost in a cloud of dust.

Brittany curled tighter in a ball on the rickety motel bed and moaned. She raised her head just enough to read the time on the travel clock. Four o'clock.

"Oh, lord," she whispered.

Cramps. Of all things to have happen. It rankled her that they hit her today. She'd felt great earlier. In fact, she'd jumped out of bed and after slipping into her shorts, T-shirt and running shoes, had asked directions for a jogging route.

She'd gone to the high school track and run three miles. The cramping had started shortly afterward. Her day had gone from tolerable to terrible.

No way could she face Matt in this condition, she told herself. She tried to call him, but he didn't answer. She had swallowed a couple of over-the-counter painkillers and gone to bed. She was still there.

She knew Matt wondered where she was. On second thought, she doubted that. She'd probably made his day by *not* showing up.

She curled even tighter into her ball as her thoughts turned chaotic. How had things gotten so out of hand? When had things gotten so personal? What was it about him? she kept asking herself. Why couldn't she treat him like her other clients?

He wasn't like other men. From the moment she'd seen Matt, she'd been aware of him on a different level—his dark face, his taut body, the heat that radiated from him, and the scent of his skin, a scent that was all his own...

Suddenly Brittany sat up and watched the room spin. That was preferable to thinking wayward thoughts about Matt Diamond. Anyhow, she was making a mountain out of a molehill.

What she needed to do was return to his place one more time so she could complete her report, make her judgment, then get out of this godforsaken place.

But not today. She couldn't face him today.

She sat up and realized she wasn't sick to her stomach. Courageously, she stood. Maybe if she brushed her teeth and showered, she might feel like eating something. She suspected hunger was contributing to her light-headedness.

When she was halfway to the bathroom, the phone rang. Matt, she thought. She stiffened, then relaxed. He didn't know where she was staying.

She dismissed him from her mind, backtracked and lifted the receiver.

"Hello."

"It's me, Wade."

Brittany eased onto the side of the bed. "Hi. I was going to report in today."

"That's not why I'm calling."

"Oh?"

"Your old man wanted me to check on you."

Brittany brightened. "He did?"

"Yeah," Wade said. "He's feeling a little under the weather."

"What's wrong?" Alarm was in her voice.

"Just a cold and sore throat. Nothing serious. I just think he wants you back to pamper him."

Brittany doubted that, but she didn't say it out loud. "I hope to wind things up here tomorrow or the next day."

"Is everything all right?" Wade asked.

You mean you care enough to ask? she wanted to say, but didn't. "Yes, of course it is."

"Well, you don't sound like it," Wade said bluntly. "I smell trouble. I was counting on you to nail this guy."

"I told you I can handle it. Now, if there's nothing else . . ." she added pointedly.

"I hope your mood improves when you do come back." With that Wade hung up.

"Goodbye to you, too," Brittany said, and dropped the receiver onto the hook.

The second round of medicine had taken effect. She felt that she could face the world, especially after she put some food into her stomach. She knew where she was going, too.

Annie's Padlock.

That's a name for the record book, she thought as she stepped into the shower. She'd noticed the place, a rambling wooden building surrounded by dozens of cars every time she passed it. At first she hadn't known what it was because the name hadn't identified it. But then she'd gotten a whiff of the aroma and knew.

Last evening, she'd mentioned Annie's Padlock to the motel clerk.

"Is the food as good there as it smells?" she asked.

The clerk, a young scrawny boy in his late teens, paled as his eyes pursued her, taking in her perfectly made up face, her designer linen suit and pumps. Then he flushed as if embarrassed by his actions.

"Oh, yes . . . I mean, no, ma'am," he stammered.

Brittany's lips twitched. "Exactly which is it?"

"Oh, the food's real good, but the crowd—er—gets a little rough sometimes." He frowned. "You know what I mean," he added rather primly.

Brittany's lips burgeoned into a full-fledged smile. "I certainly do."

He looked relieved. "It's just that I don't think you'd be comfortable there. I know another place much more suitable to your taste." His face brightened. "You like German food? There's a wonderful place out on Highway 94 . . ."

Wonderful or not, Brittany wasn't interested in German food. With a lingering smile, she set about making herself presentable.

She walked outside and saw that the sun had set. She paused and looked up. The sky was streaked with colors. That was a good omen, she told herself. And so was Annie's Padlock. It was definitely the antidote she needed to revive her spirits.

And make her forget Matthew Diamond.

Seven

Matt pulled into the parking lot of Annie's Padlock much later than he had intended. After he'd left the house, he'd remembered he needed a part for his truck. The parts place hadn't been that far out of the way, so he'd opted to stop there first. He'd purchased the part and was about to step into his pickup when a fellow logger had hollered at him.

They had chatted a while, mainly about Matt's recent troubles.

As he got out of the truck and walked into the café, he adjusted his eyes to the dimness. Still he saw her. Right off.

His stride broke abruptly. He stared, then blinked, certain Brittany was a mirage, that his eyes were playing a dirty trick on him.

Matt opened them again. Wider. No tricks. No mirage. She sat at a table in a secluded corner of the cozy dining room. Suddenly everything else around him became of secondary importance. He didn't notice that business was slow, that only a few other couples occupied tables or that the counter was occupied by three men who were also watching every move that Brittany made.

He couldn't say what song was playing on the jukebox, either, or identify the heavenly smell that drifted from the kitchen.

A cup of coffee occupied the place mat directly in front of her, and she slowly trailed a long fingernail around its rim. Her eyes had a faraway, dazed expression in them. But underneath those eyes were dark shadows that reminded him of faint bruises. And her face had a slightly drawn look to it.

Those slight imperfections enhanced her refined features. She wore a pair of jeans—tight-fitting, he bet—and a turquoise cotton shirt. Her red hair, complemented by the color of her shirt, was loose and windblown, the style that urged a man to run his fingers through it.

But it wasn't her hair that held his attention; it was her breasts, which were boldly outlined by the fit of her shirt. He imagined they were perfection personified and wondered...

Rage invaded his bloodstream. Yet he couldn't take his eyes off her. Sexually, she stirred him more, made him more aware of her than any woman he'd ever known.

And while that weakness played a big part in his fury, it wasn't all of it. He was livid because she was here—when she'd stood him up.

He fought for control. She hadn't seen him, which was definitely in his favor.

"Hiya, Matt," a blond-haired waitress said softly as she passed in front of him, carrying a tray loaded with food.

Matt tipped his hat and smiled, though the smile never reached his eyes. "Hello, Mandy."

Another waitress walked up to Brittany's table and said something, something that Matt couldn't decipher. But he heard Brittany's laugh, and the throaty sound further assaulted his senses.

"Are you eating tonight or drinking?" Mandy asked, giving him a perplexed look.

Matt barely heard her. He had thoughts only for Brittany. "Er...what?"

The waitress sucked in her lower lip and said in a pouting voice, "Whatsa matter with you tonight, honey? You look all tensed up." She winked at him and broadened her smile. "I betcha I can make whatever's bothering you better."

Matt sighed. Her come-on to him was a seemingly endless ritual. "I'll have a beer," he said tightly. Usually he played along with her banter. Sometimes he even egged her on—though they both knew they'd never sleep together—but it got him more heaping platefuls of food.

Her face momentarily lost its animation, but she rebounded with a cooed, "All rightie." She sidled up to him and whispered, "Maybe next time, huh?"

"Yeah, next time," Matt murmured. Her response failed to register.

He moved toward Brittany's table. Halfway there, heat surged up the back of his throat. He swallowed against it. He cursed silently, then stepped up to her table.

As if she knew she was no longer alone, Brittany whipped around. Startled, her green eyes widened.

"Surprise, surprise." Matt's gaze drilled her.

Brittany stiffened and opened her mouth. Before she could say anything, Matt spoke in a low, terse voice. "Just what the hell are you doing here?"

"I think that should be fairly obvious," she said, her tone biting.

He ignored her bad attitude. "Well, this is no place for you to be, that's for damn sure."

Brittany didn't seem in the least intimidated. That added fuel to his anger. The muscles along his cheek and jaw stood out in rigid cords. "I waited all afternoon for you to show up."

A small crease appeared between her eyebrows. "I know, and I'm sorry." Her voice was husky.

"Is that all you have to say?"

"Look, I wasn't feeling good, okay?"

Matt snorted.

Her eyes glazed over. "Look, I fell asleep and when I woke up, it was too late. I tried to call..."

"Knowing that I wouldn't be in the house?" He heard the tremble of rage in his voice, but he couldn't control it. "That's a lousy excuse, and you know it. I want that damn claim finished and settled. You hear me?"

She stared at him openmouthed, and her eyes were building up to a blaze.

"Hey, fellow."

At the sound of the unfamiliar voice, both Brittany and Matt swung around.

A man dressed in a dark brown business suit stood next to Matt. He was every bit as tall as Matt and about his size and weight. But he'd been drinking, heavily. His breath was so bad that Matt stepped back.

The man grinned.

"Do I know you?" Matt asked, not amused.

The man swayed slightly, then grinned again, only this time at Brittany.

"Is this fellow bothering you, little lady?"

Brittany opened her mouth to reply. Matt interrupted. "Butt out, mister."

The man hiccuped. "Oh, no. You butt out."

Something in Matt's eyes turned savage. "I think you'd best—"

The man leaned toward Matt. "I had my eye on her a long time before you came in, my friend."

"I'm not your friend," Matt said. If the man hadn't been so far gone, he would have picked up on the steel in Matt's voice. "And I said get lost."

"Matt..." Brittany rose and placed a hand on his arm. Her face was clouded with anxiety. "Matt... don't. Let it go. He's harmless."

"That's right, honey. You tell him. What do you say you and me split and—"

He never knew what hit him.

Matt doubled his fist and delivered an uppercut square in the middle of the man's chin. For a second, he stared at Matt as if he couldn't believe what had happened. Then he fell backward and crashed into the table behind him. Dishes and glassware flew like tiny missiles around the room.

Matt watched, his face expressionless, as the stranger finally hit the floor with the grace of a lump of wet cement.

The entire room went graveyard quiet. No one moved. No one said a word. They just stared. Then everyone began talking at once.

Still the cold-cocked stranger did not so much as twitch from his sprawled position on the floor.

"Oh, my God," Brittany whispered, raising horrified, accusing eyes to Matt.

"See, didn't I tell you it was a mistake coming here?"

"How...how could you?" There was the smallest break in her voice, and her lower lip quivered.

Not out of fear, Matt told himself, but out of rage, rage as potent as his had been moments before. He had embarrassed her. Yeah, his backwoods antics had embarrassed the high-and-mighty Brittany Fleming.

Her next words bore out his thoughts.

"You're...you're nothing but...savage." Brittany grabbed her purse, whirled and walked past him with her head slightly in the air.

He would have charged after her, but Mandy placed a hand on his arm and stared into his face. Her eyes shone. "That was real nice, honey, real nice. I wish I had someone to do that for me."

Matt shook off her hand, his eyes on the door that Brittany had just exited. "Ask Harry to haul this piece of garbage out for me, will you?"

He strode out the door.

The parking lot was half empty and well lit. Finding her was easy.

She was trying to put her key in the lock when he reached her. "Brittany," he said softly, so as not to frighten her.

"Stay away from me!" she cried, twisting to face him. "Haven't you already done enough damage?"

"Keep your voice down, for god's sake!" His heart pounded, and he smelled the electricity of his own frustration as it shorted out.

"Go away, damn you." She turned to get into the car.

Without thinking, Matt grabbed her arm. "Oh, no, you don't."

Her gaze dipped to his hand, which surrounded her arm, then up to meet his fixed look. "Do you always solve everything by using he-man tactics?"

It wasn't so much what she said that sent his temper over the edge, but the way she said it, with that contemptuous lilt in her voice. He hauled her against his chest. The sudden whimper that rushed through her lips made him realize what he was doing. Still he didn't release her. His hand froze around her delicate arm.

Their eyes met and held.

The air hummed between them; it vibrated with a raw tension.

"Matt . . . please."

She felt it, too. He heard it in her voice. Saw it in her eyes.

His anger deserted him. But not the heat. It accentuated the warm, muggy night. He should never have come after her. He regretted it—especially now, alone with her, with this sultry throb in the air.

Yet he was powerless to rectify his mistake. He couldn't move. His legs felt disconnected from his body. His breath caught, as if his lungs had iced up.

He wanted her. God, he wanted her. Now. He could taste those damp, perfect lips, feel an aroused nipple against the palm of his hand...

"Matt..." Brittany's cry was a breathless whisper.

He leaned forward, only to suddenly hear a warning bell go off in his brain. What the hell was he doing? Exactly what he swore he wouldn't do.

He let her go, suddenly and without mercy.

Brittany swayed, and if her car hadn't been behind her, she would have lost her balance. He dared not touch her, not even to steady her.

He turned, posed to walk away. She grabbed his arm. The muscles bunched under her light touch.

"Matt..."

"No...don't. Don't say another word." He took several steps.

"Where are you going?"

He stopped, swung around, his features contorted. "Going? Where am I going?"

She flinched under his cutting words.

"I'm going inside—alone."

The phone rang at five-thirty.

Brittany sat up in the bed like she'd been shot. The

phone rang twice before she realized that the offensive sound was indeed the phone.

She slapped the receiver several times before she got it to her ear. "Hello," she mumbled.

"Ms. Fleming, this is the front desk. I have a message for you."

Brittany sat up straighter. "What is it?"

"A Mr. Howard Hickman called and said that your father was in the hospital, but that he is better."

Brittany fought down the panic. "When...did I get the message?" If only she could think. Her mind refused to function. But she wasn't surprised. After last night and that round with Matt...

"A few moments ago."

"Excuse me?"

The clerk drew a deep breath. "A few minutes ago," he repeated.

"I heard that, but I don't understand."

"I rang your room, but there was no answer. I decided to try again on the chance I'd gotten the wrong room the first time."

"I see. Well, thank you very much."

"You're welcome." A pause. "Will you be checking out, ma'am? If so, I could have your bill ready and waiting."

Brittany didn't hesitate. "Yes, please. But I'll be returning, and if this room is still available, I'd like it back."

"No problem."

She kept her hand on the receiver long after the conversation ended. She decided not to call the hospital; she would go there instead.

But she did have to call Matt and tell him she wouldn't be seeing him today, either. Maybe he wouldn't be expecting her. After last night...

She wouldn't think about last night. Not now. She couldn't bear it. Sooner or later, though, she was going to have to face the fact that, crazy or not, an attraction was there, sharp and deep.

Then she was going to have to decide what to do about it. But not now. First she had to call Matt.

When she lifted the receiver a second time, she noticed her hand was shaking.

Eight

"Howard's exactly right for you."

"Daddy..." Brittany had heard this argument a hundred times and didn't want to hear it again, especially not while trapped with her daddy in his hospital suite.

"Don't you 'daddy' me, young lady," Walter responded, his mouth a grim line. "I know what's best for you."

Brittany swallowed a sigh and turned away. Her eyes locked on the painting on the wall. The artwork was gaudy, she thought inanely, even though it had cost several thousand dollars.

But then everything in here had cost money. Nothing but the best for her daddy. And why not? He was a wealthy man who enjoyed—demanded—the best of everything.

He also demanded that everyone adopt his opinions and ideas. If he said it, it was right. But it was Brittany who caught the brunt of this self-indulgence. Today she didn't need the grief.

Her nerves felt burned out already—ever since she'd called Matt. A shiver ran through her as she thought about the sound of his deep voice, thought about *him*.

The phone conversation had transpired as predicted. He'd been broodingly uncommunicative. She had known what was on his mind—their close encounter in the parking lot. And when she'd told him she couldn't keep the appointment, he'd become fiercely angry. But then she'd explained about her daddy being in the hospital, and his tone had softened somewhat.

"Brittany, I wish you'd pay attention when I'm talking to you."

"Sorry, Daddy," Brittany muttered hastily. "I don't love Howard, and you're going to have to accept that."

"It's time you were settled. And love's not everything." Walter shifted positions in the bed, and when he did, it brought on another coughing spell.

The rattling in his chest was so severe, Brittany winced. "See what you've done?" she said, rushing to his side and reaching for a glass of water.

When he was less red-faced and seemingly in control once again, she added, "I didn't come home to hear a lecture—I came to check on you, to make sure you were all right. And from the looks of things, you're no better.'' She smiled and tried to eject some humor into her voice. ''If someone were listening to us, they'd think you wanted to get rid of me.''

''You know better than that. It's just that I know what's best for you.''

''Daddy—''

''All right,'' Walter interrupted, ''I won't say anymore. But promise me you'll give it some thought.'' His eyes darkened. ''I won't even entertain the idea of you marrying beneath yourself.''

She didn't argue. Her daddy was a snob, a bigger snob than any woman she knew. And when he was in one of his moods, she couldn't reason with him.

''When do you think you'll be dismissed?'' Brittany asked lightly, changing the subject.

Walter flexed his lips. ''Today, I hope. I have so much work to do.''

''How can you think of work when you're lying here with double pneumonia?''

''That's nothing. I'm going to be fine.'' He flashed her a sharp look. ''Speaking of work, how's it going with that logging fellow?''

Brittany pushed a strand of hair out of her eyes. ''I'm about to bring my investigation to a close.''

His features brightened. ''Need any help or advice?''

''No. I'm handling it on my own, thank you.''

For a second, Brittany thought she detected a glimmer of admiration in his eyes, but if she did, it faded instantly. The hard look returned.

''Well, see that you rule in our favor.''

''Even if it's not right?''

"You know better than that." Walter's tone was clipped.

"When I'm done, I'm sure you'll get a copy of the report."

"You might as well tend to business, because I don't need you here."

His harsh dismissal cut into her heart like a sharp knife. There was no defense against it.

"I guess I'll be on my way," she said around the lump in her throat.

A few minutes later she walked outside and breathed in the fresh spring air. Her spirits lifted instantly, only to have them suddenly hit rock bottom.

This afternoon she had to face Matt.

"Billy?"

Matt was almost to the workshop when he saw a figure move behind the skidder.

"Yeah, it's me," Billy said, moving into the open.

"What the hell do you think you're doing?"

Billy pawed the dirt with the toe of his boot. "Waitin' on you. Hopin' you'd have work for me."

Matt didn't like him hanging around his place. But then, considering the trouble he'd had, he didn't like *anyone* hanging around.

"How long you been here?" he asked, not bothering to curb his irritation.

Billy looked away from Matt's intense scrutiny. "Not long," he mumbled.

"It just so happens I can use you today."

His sulky features cleared. "Oh, really?"

"Yeah. You ready to go?"

Billy scratched his head vigorously. He eyed Matt carefully. "Ready when you are."

"As soon as Elmer gets here, we'll go."

Matt turned his back on the kid and wondered what there was about Billy Frost that raised his hackles.

They both heard the car. But it was Elmer who looked up. He chuckled. "You've got company, boss."

Matt groaned. "Company? That's the last damn thing I need. Who is it?"

"I'm thinking it's that insurance dame."

"Brittany?"

"Whatever."

Matt looked up, then swore. It had been a long, hot day in the woods, and the last thing he needed was Brittany prancing her tight little butt around here as if she owned the place.

Besides, he was stunned that she would show up again. He fully expected her to send someone else. Again he should've known better.

"It's her, all right."

"You wanna call it a day?" Elmer asked.

Matt wiped the grease off his hands, then tossed the rag aside. "What I want is for you to wipe that chicken-eating grin off your face."

Elmer's grin merely widened. "Anything you say, boss."

Matt glared at him.

Elmer raised his hands in self-defense. "I'll just plan to see you in the morning."

"Yeah, okay," Matt said absently. He watched Brittany park her car under a big oak tree.

Elmer picked up his lunch pail and crossed to his pickup. "By the way, you know how I feel about that Frost kid—don't trust that little weasel—but I'll have to admit he sure as hell came in handy today."

"I know. And I was glad I could work him. Still, I feel guilty—"

"Don't. You can't help this run of bad luck."

"Thanks," Matt said, and watched broodingly as Elmer cranked his pickup and drove off.

He switched his attention to Brittany. She had gotten out of the car and was walking toward him, pad and pencil in hand. She looked wonderful, he thought, conscious of his own dirty appearance.

Her hair was curlier than usual, her clothes brighter. Or maybe it was the raspberry-colored blouse and matching pants she had on. With her hair, they made a contrasting but powerful statement. He waited for his senses to stop reeling.

"I hope you don't mind my showing up like this," she said in her husky voice, now slightly strained, as if she were again remembering Annie's Padlock.

He knew he damn sure was. Right now he was having difficulty catching his breath.

"Matt?"

"Er...I don't mind if it'll speed things up." His voice was ragged as a bread knife.

"This will only take a minute. I need the information on the stolen truck."

"You could've gotten that over the phone," he said in what he hoped was a neutral tone. Had she wanted to see him as much as he wanted to see her? Or was he misreading her entirely?

"I need a picture, if you have one."

"I see," he said suddenly, harshly. So much for his thoughts. "Well, you've wasted your time. I don't have one."

Brittany scribbled that down. "I have a few more questions."

"You want to go inside?"

"No. That's...er...not necessary. I know you're tired...." Her voice played out, and she lowered her eyes. She couldn't seem to take his penetrating look another minute.

"Okay, shoot."

"I need the make, model, color, serial number, et cetera."

"It'll take me a few minutes to get them."

"I'll wait."

Swallowing an expletive, Matt turned and trudged inside the house. When he returned with the information, she took it from him at the same time as she asked another question.

"Where was the truck? In the woods or here?"

He stared at her a long moment, though he refused to look beyond the V at the neck of her blouse. The mood he was in, he didn't dare look lower. But he knew what was there. He'd memorized the way her breasts had thrust against the fabric of her clothing when she moved—as if they ached to be free....

"Here," he said quickly.

"Show me where."

They walked to the shed.

"Who saw it last?"

"Me." Matt pointed to the exact spot. "I parked it there."

"Did the sheriff find a different set of tire tracks?"

"Yep." Matt leaned against the building and stared at her from under the brim of his Stetson. "So far, though, he hasn't tracked them down."

"I understand that sometimes stolen equipment is taken to the border and sold."

"Ah, so you have been doing your homework?"

"That's right," she said pleasantly, as if he'd complimented her instead of insulting her.

He tried to stifle the impulse to ruffle that calm, but he didn't succeed. "That's one possibility," he said. "Another one is that other loggers simply don't want to buy their own equipment. So they steal."

"That's crazy."

"Crazy or not, it happens." He paused. "So when will I know?"

"Soon."

He snorted. "Surely you can do better than that."

"Not at the moment."

"Anything else, then?" he asked pointedly.

"No." She avoided his eyes. "I'll be in touch."

He stood quietly while she got into the car. But it took all his effort to stand still, especially when his thoughts were so chaotic.

He tried to keep his voice expressionless, but he failed miserably. "Is that it? You'll be in touch?" A scraping sound punctuated each word.

Brittany faced him. "For now."

Anger struck him again. He felt it like a tangible thing. "You're enjoying this, aren't you?"

"I don't know what you're talking about," she said coolly.

"Oh, I think you do. You love having me at your mercy."

"That's not true," she replied in her haughtiest voice.

He ignored her as if she hadn't spoken. "It won't always be that way, you know."

"Is that a threat?"

He looked her up and down. "What do you think?"

His words shattered her artificial composure. She jerked open her car door, got inside and slammed it.

"I'll be back when I have my report." Her voice was as frigid as her posture.

"Yeah. Sure. You do that."

The second she heard the pickup, Brittany got out of her car. Matt pulled up beside her and got out of his pickup.

She couldn't help but notice how good he looked, even though he needed a shower and shave in the worst way. Yet when he stopped within touching distance of her, he didn't smell offensive. The scent of pine and sweat was an overwhelmingly familiar combination. She went weak.

"I...er...began to think you weren't coming home," she said.

His expression said clearly, "Not you again." But when he spoke, his tone was even. "Oh, and just why is that?"

"You're so late," Brittany said matter-of-factly, looking at him in only brief, lateral glances. "I've been waiting quite a while."

Matt removed his dusty hat and slapped it against his leg. "You should've told me you were coming."

"I didn't know myself."

His eyes were smoky. "We had some delays."

Brittany ran a tongue across her lower lip. "I'm sorry. About the delays, I mean," she added, a slight huskiness to her tone.

"It happens," he said, his eye intent on her face. "So what are you doing here?"

"You know the answer to that."

"Yeah, I guess I do."

"I've finished my report." She forced her expression not to show the turmoil his presence created within her.

"So, the verdict's in, huh?"

"The verdict's in." Brittany's response was soft.

He didn't reply.

"Do you mind if I come in?" The words slipped out in a controlled rush.

"I have to take a shower."

"Is that a yes?"

"If you don't mind watching, it is."

"I don't mind."

Their eyes met. There was an element of raw emotion in the air.

"Suit yourself," Matt muttered. He motioned for her to precede him up the porch.

Brittany paused just inside the door, her eyes scanning the room. "Nice."

And it was. The room had highly polished wood flooring, and was paneled in a light-hued wood, which made it seem larger than it actually was. A sofa and matching chair hugged a large area rug at one end. An entertainment center and fireplace dominated the remaining walls.

Pictures and other personal memorabilia were scattered around. It was uncluttered, but warm.

Brittany turned toward him. "It suits you, you know."

He smirked. "I'm glad the lady approves."

"I wasn't being insulting."

He gave a tired sigh. "I know."

They stared at each other for a long moment. Finally Matt said, "Make yourself comfortable. I won't be long."

But Brittany couldn't get comfortable. She was too uptight. She longed to be through with this so that she could get back home, back to the safety of her world. Not only was she afraid of Matt, but she was afraid of herself because of the way he made her feel.

She was still trying to analyze her thoughts when he walked through the door, dressed in jeans and a shirt. But the shirt was open. Her eyes dipped to his chest where water clung to the tips of his hair and sparkled like tiny diamonds.

"So let's have it," he said thickly, as if responding to the look in her eyes.

"You don't want to sit down?" she asked uneasily.

"No, but you're welcome to."

"No, I'll just stand."

"Look, let's just cut to the chase, okay?"

"All . . . right."

"So when am I going to get my money?"

"You're not."

He uncoiled himself and took a menacing step closer to her. "Explain that."

"I think you're sabotaging your own equipment, and I intend to prove it."

Nine

Matt stiffened. Every line in his face was sculpted in fury. "What did you say?"

She shrugged, but it was to hide a shudder. "You know what I said. But I'll repeat it anyway. After giving my report careful consideration, I have concluded that you deliberately—"

His smile was lethal, a deadly weapon. And it stopped her cold. "You're crazy as hell!"

"You're entitled to your opinion, of course," Brittany said stiffly, averting her eyes.

He stepped closer, until he was so close he towered over her. Her eyes widened, but she held her ground.

Fury shot through him. His shoulders tensed, and his hands clenched until his knuckles turned white. He willed himself to relax—to fight her accusation. He couldn't. He lowered his shoulders and shifted positions so that she couldn't see he was too furious to uncurl them.

"You think you're so damn smart, don't you?"

Brittany drew a slow breath. "Look, I don't like this any more than you do, but the facts are just that—facts. And I can't ignore them."

"You can't ignore them!" His lips twisted around the words. "That's the best yet. Oh, yeah, that's really the best."

"Try to understand our side."

He made an ugly, disbelieving noise in his throat. "You don't have a side! Not as far as I'm concerned." He had difficulty breathing. "I've paid my insurance premiums when I couldn't pay anything else, and by god, you're going to keep your end of the bargain!"

He heard her choke, saw her face tighten, but when she spoke, her tone was steady. "You can't threaten me. I have the last say. And until this is settled, there won't be a check."

Matt couldn't take any more. "Just be quiet, okay!" His eyes turned into icy chips. "You don't know the first thing about logging. You're just a spoiled brat who's window dressing for Daddy—"

Her hand acted with a mind of its own. That had to be the case, otherwise she would not have dared hit him. But her hand shot out and struck him hard across his right cheekbone.

Brittany gasped. "How dare you talk to me like that!"

Her holier-than-thou attitude set him off like an electric charge. He lunged forward.

"No!" A panicky whisper. "Don't touch me!"

If she had said something else, he would never have acted. She was within her rights to slap his face for that last remark. It was not only uncalled for, but out of line as well. She wasn't the type who would accept such an insult. But it was the way she said it, as if she couldn't stand for him to put his dirty hands on her.

Not to touch her. Impossible, especially since every time she came near him, he'd ached to do exactly that.

He grasped her wrist and jerked her against him. Her breasts collided with his chest, and her legs slapped his thighs. They were so close, he could feel his hot breath bounce off her forehead. But he didn't relinquish his hold. He was past the point of no return. He didn't care that he was hurting her; he tightened his stranglehold.

"Let me go," she cried, struggling against him.

"Be still!" His voice was guttural, almost inhuman.

Her moist lips opened, partly from pain, partly from anger. That unconscious gesture, combined with her body squirming against him, sent him over the edge.

Matt lowered his head and claimed her mouth. He ground his hard lips into her soft ones, and with his hands in her hair, held her head in position.

She stopped struggling. He nudged her lips apart and touched her tongue. It was as if time had stopped; they seemed suspended in space.

Matt's breath ran out; he let her go. Silence, like a vacuum, fell around them. He didn't move, fully expecting to feel the sting of her hand across his face again.

Instead, she gripped his arms. Strong nails dug into his biceps. A tiny sound erupted from deep within her throat. Tears darkened her eyes and clumped in her lashes. With trembling fingers she circled his neck and firmly drew his head down to hers.

Their lips met this time with such fierce suddenness that his legs felt like rubber bands, and his heart pounded in his chest.

He tore his mouth from hers, then massaged it across her cheek.

"Please . . . don't," he whispered in her ear. His breathing came in short, gusty spurts. "Don't do this. Don't play with me like this. You make me crazy. You have from the first day we met." He seared her skin again, then sank his hot, moist mouth into hers.

Brittany couldn't say a word, couldn't respond to his gut-wrenching confession. She felt as if she were dangling off the edge of a cliff. Yet the pressure of his body against hers was real, exquisitely real.

She clung to him, rising and falling with the rhythm of his kisses, and felt the tension break inside her with the force of a tropical current slicing through a formidable ice floe. She clung even tighter to the back of his neck, as if controlled by another being.

She had never lost herself before now.

His budding hardness situated itself between her legs. She gasped as she felt him like hot iron through the second skin of her pants. His hands found their way inside her shirt and cupped a breast while he covered her mouth with his—forcefully, as if to devour her.

The thrust, the taste of his tongue generated an all-consuming heat. His hair was thick and coarse beneath her fingers, but tough and resilient, like the rest of him.

Without breaking contact with his protruding hardness, Brittany stroked his back and felt his taut muscles bunch. She wanted more and pressed harder against him.

He moaned, shifted to cup her buttocks and lifted her to her toes. Her body arched instinctively, supported by his strength.

While their lips continued to feast on each other with desperate, greedy kisses, she tried to run her hands over his chest, but his shirt was in the way. She clawed at it, freed it from his jeans, then ran her fingernails up and down his spine.

"Oh, yes," he panted.

Brittany felt his shiver, especially when she ran her hands possessively over the hard ridges of his bronzed flesh, smooth and hot to the touch. Only it wasn't enough to feel his flesh; she wanted to taste it, too. She brought her lips to his chest. She sought out and found one pebble-hard nipple. She tongued it until the tremors shuddered through him.

"Oh, God, you're forcing me to die a slow death." His voice was pleading as his tongue slid between her lips. He ravaged the delicate contours of her mouth. "I want . . . you . . ."

Her nipples tightened and ached with need. "Show me!" she whispered, equally frantically, dampening his neck with open lips and a darting tongue.

"Yes."

The tiny word came out a murmur, sounding both harsh and soft at once.

With the same impatience Brittany had shown him, he tore her blouse open. The expensive buttons popped off and flew in different directions. The blouse came next. It surrounded her ankles as he moved to her bra. One jerk of the front snap and the bra was open, then off.

His hands felt like nubby silk on her firm, naked breasts. He moaned when he saw her distended nipples. His head dipped, and his lips closed around the tip of one breast.

But his eyes sought hers. There was fear there as surely as there was hunger.

His hunger won. He undid the button at the waistband of her slacks. Within seconds, she was naked and pressed against him urgently, yearning to feel the warmth that came from skin against skin.

But that couldn't be until he was as naked as she. Feverishly, she reached for the snap at his jeans.

He steeled her hands and said thickly, "No. Let me. It's faster."

His clothes joined hers. His pupils dilated, and he reached for her. His hands were everywhere at once, all over her body. She felt invaded; heat like nothing she'd ever felt before shot through her body, settled at the core of her, caused her to throb.

She wanted him. She wanted all of him—with a wanton ferociousness that stunned her. How could this be happening? What kind of passion was this that erupted so wildly? Shameless, that was what it was. But this desire for him had simmered just below the surface all along. Now it burst wide open, with the impact of a broken dam, making her strong and weak at the same time.

His callused hands slid down her back and surrounded the cheeks of her bare buttocks. She opened her mouth to cry out. He stifled that cry with his lips, eased a hand down and slipped a finger inside her. She contracted, then shuddered within the circle of his arms.

He lifted her off her feet and said roughly, "Lock your legs around me."

"Matt!"

"Sh. Just do it!"

She did, and he backed her against the wall. Her thighs were liquid fire, enabling him to enter her swiftly, completely, hotly. He latched onto a breast with his lips and sucked; every nerve in her body shrieked.

His thrusts were forceful and deep, and she wanted this sweet pain never to end, despite the fact she was being swept away by something she didn't understand.

Oh, she cried silently into his shoulder.

He groaned, then strained against her even more, giving her all of him in one final thrust.

Their moans came simultaneously. When it was over, his lips sought her pulse at the base of her throat and listened to its endless message.

While he was still inside her, slowly stiffening again, Brittany felt his eyes on her.

A crescent moon flanked by brilliant stars made this possible. Its beam poured through the window and was his guiding light.

Somehow they had made it to his bedroom. Brittany didn't know how, didn't know when, but that wasn't important. The important things was that they were locked in another embrace.

No words had been spoken; none were spoken now. None were necessary. They were caught in the silence; like a third being, it pulsed around them.

With an unsteady hand, he pushed her damp hair out of her face and began to move gently, creating a friction that again threatened to set her on fire.

He was tender, giving, and, at the very end, she couldn't be certain, but she thought she felt a tear drop.

Stillness. Their breathing and the sound of two hearts in tune.

Half awake, Brittany moved her legs, then winced. The sharp jab of pain caused her eyes to pop open. She stared at the strange ceiling and groped for her bearings. Where was she? And why was she so stiff, so sore?

She scanned the room. When she spied the Stetson hanging on the back of a rocker, she froze. Her heart plummeted as if in a crashing elevator.

"Oops!" she said raggedly, knowing instantly what she had done.

Her teeth began to chatter, and nothing would stop them, not even biting down on her lower lip until she tasted blood. She wouldn't panic. But oh, God, she wanted to. She wanted to scream in anger at herself.

Instead, she climbed out of bed and, dragging the sheet with her, tiptoed out of the bedroom, down the hall and into the kitchen. She knew she was alone; the house was just too silent. Yet she had to be sure.

The note in the middle of the kitchen table was propped against the salt and pepper shakers. The words were printed and large enough for her to read from where she stood.

"Make yourself at home. I'll see you later, and we'll take up where we left off. Matt."

Brittany gripped the door facing for support. Her face turned bright red, then deathly white. Not only was she mortified at what she had allowed to happen—but she was more mortified that he would assume she'd do it again.

She grabbed her stomach in hopes of retaining its contents. She'd pulled some idiotic stunts in her life, but this one was the worst. There was no excuse for her behavior.

She refused to give in to the tears that burned her eyes, and turned to hurry to the bedroom.

Five minutes later, she was out the door and out of Matt Diamond's life. Forever.

Ten

"**W**ay to go."

Brittany sneezed into the tissue before she faced her boss, who had eased a hip down on one corner of her desk. "The case is not over yet." Her tone registered fatigue.

"True, but it looks like you've nailed him."

"We'll see."

Wade shoved his glasses closer to the bridge of his nose, then frowned. "What do you mean, we'll see? Why, from reading your report, it's obvious we caught Diamond with his fingers in the cookie jar."

Brittany shuddered, though not outwardly, she hoped. Anything and everything about Matt affected her like that. His name spoken aloud, his name written on a piece of paper—it didn't matter.

Wade cocked his head. "You got a dilly of a cold, don't you?"

"Sinus infection, actually," Brittany said, getting up from her desk and walking to the window. She looked into the overcast sky. The bottom was going to drop out any moment now. She didn't mind; the weather matched her mood. Dreary.

"Is that why you didn't return to the Diamond place?"

Brittany's hesitation turned into a long silence.

"Brittany, I'm talking to you, for god's sake."

"I'm sorry," she said, turning from the window and giving him her full attention. "No, that's not why. Although this mess did hit me the minute I got back home."

"So what's the reason?" He removed his glasses and blew on one lens. "I thought this case was your baby."

She walked to the coffeemaker near her desk and poured a generous cup. She held her cup out to Wade. "Would you care for some?"

"No, thanks," he said impatiently, as if he resented anything that interfered with their conversation. "Just answer the question."

"It's still my baby, as you put it." Brittany averted her eyes and ran an index finger around the edge of her cup. "But I saw no reason to return, especially after Bruce offered to see that the equipment was hauled to the nearest repair shop so it could be analyzed. After all, he knows more about that than I do."

"I can't believe you'd admit that."

His sarcasm went right by her. "While we wait, I'm going to get started on the Hanover case."

"Well, if those shade tree mechanics in most small towns run true to form, it'll be a couple more weeks until we get their report. They're usually slower than molasses running uphill."

Brittany blew on her coffee, then took a sip. "I was hoping we'd hear much sooner. How come it takes so long?"

"Their tardiness plays into our hands, actually. We caution them not to hurry. When you suspect sabotage, you have to make damn sure you've covered all the bases."

Brittany set her cup down and walked to her desk, her heels sinking into the plush carpet. "He's going to give us trouble." Her voice faltered slightly.

Wade fixed her with a baleful eye. "And that bothers you?"

"No, no it doesn't," Brittany said hurriedly. "It's just that—" She broke off, unwilling to go on.

Wade fiddled with his paisley tie and smiled a cocky smile. "He's on our timetable now. We got him. And you know yourself, it takes at least thirty to sixty days to wrap up a case like this. Maybe longer, if we want to drag it out, which would be to our advantage."

"In the meantime, what if he goes under?"

Wade pinned her with an odd glance. "He'll just go under. But that's not our problem. Right?"

Brittany smiled tightly. "That's right."

"You'll let me know the minute Bruce gets back."

"You'll be the second to know."

Wade stood. "You best go home and get well. First Walter, now you. Hope to hell the bug's not catching."

Brittany barely contained her agitation. A little of this man went a long way. "There's nothing to catch. Daddy had a bronchial infection, and mine's sinus."

"It never hurts to be careful," Wade said as he made his way to the door. He paused and turned. "I'll have to tell you, I didn't think you had it in you."

"What?" she asked, though she didn't really care.

"Going for Diamond's jugular and winning."

"I wouldn't celebrate just yet, Wade. The case isn't closed. We have to *prove* Diamond's at fault."

"We will," he said airily, then closed the door behind him.

Brittany fought the urge to pick up the blotter on her desk and hurl it after him.

Inky blackness surrounded her. Yet, when she entered her condo, Brittany didn't even bother to turn on a light. She locked the door and slumped against it.

She not only felt bad physically; she was destroyed mentally. Granted, Wade had upset her. What her daddy saw in him became more of a mystery every day. Sometimes Wade could be so loathsome she could barely tolerate him. Today was one of those days.

Brittany knew she wasn't being entirely fair, though. Like he said, it was her job to go for the jugular where warranted, and in Matt's case, it had certainly been warranted.

But that didn't excuse the fiasco afterward. In her own eyes, she'd done something unforgivable. She had mixed business with pleasure.

Trying to clear her thoughts, Brittany strained to hear the rain pelting outside. It had started just as she'd left the office. But she couldn't hear anything except the drum of her heartbeat in her ears.

Had she really gone to bed with Matt? Had their bodies become one? Had he been inside her so tightly, so perfectly that she forgot everything except him and what he was doing to her? How he was making her feel?

Yes!

Even after three weeks, thoughts of that night in his arms still had the power to send her stomach to her knees. How could she have behaved so irrationally, so totally out of character? She had no answers to those agonizing questions.

Her only consolation was that she wouldn't have to face Matt again.

Yet, every time the phone or the doorbell rang, Brittany feared it might be him. Every time she walked out the door, she never failed to look over her shoulder.

She need not have worried. She knew that now. He'd made no effort to seek her out. She was sure he was as glad to be rid of her as she was him. More so.

Suddenly lightning lit up the window. Brittany bolted forward, but not before she reached for the light switch beside her.

She pressed a hand to her forehead and knew she had to get hold of herself before she lost her mind.

Mercifully, the answering machine next to the lamp caught her attention. The light was blinking. She tossed her purse and suit jacket on a chair, crossed to the couch, then punched the button on the phone device.

Two messages were from friends asking her to parties. Two were from Wade. The last one was from the doctor's office.

"Brittany, this is Joyce at Dr. Daniel's office. The doctor wanted me to call and see if the medicine he prescribed is working and if you're feeling better. Also, he'll see you tomorrow at the time you asked for."

Brittany turned off the machine, eased back on the couch and looked around the room. Any other time, she might have felt the sense of pride and peace she always felt when she surveyed her domain. She had bought and decorated her condo herself. White, peach and green were the colors she carried throughout; they blended perfectly with the pickled oak hardwood floor in the living and kitchen areas and the carpet in the rooms upstairs.

However, the message from the doctor's office had destroyed any sense of well-being. It reminded her that her infection was not any better and that she had to see him in person.

Only that wasn't the real reason she had asked for an appointment. She had missed her period. The first week she hadn't been upset, attributing the lateness to nerves. But after the second week, she'd been forced to rethink that reasoning.

The alternative, of course, didn't bear thinking about. Nevertheless, it had to be faced.

Suddenly losing her nerve, Brittany rushed to the full-length mirror in her bedroom. She tried to undress, but her fingers wouldn't cooperate.

"Oh!" she said, exasperated.

Finally the task was done, and she stared at her nude body in the glass. She turned to one side, then the other, and scrutinized the slope of her slender shoulders, her high, full breasts, her flat stomach, her long, shapely legs.

Pregnant?

No. Absolutely not. Yet she *had* missed a period. She couldn't ignore that. Oh, Brittany, she thought, you stupid fool! You could be pregnant.

She reached for her robe, tied it around her, swallowed a twenty-pound lump in her throat and went slowly toward the bed. She perched on the edge. Starting with her toes, every muscle in her body jerked, one by one.

Matt Diamond's child inside her?

If there was a sphere beyond panic, she entered it.

"Are you sure you don't need anything?"

"Just your company, that's all," Maria Frost said sweetly.

Guilt stabbed Matt. He knew he should visit Maria and her son more often, despite the fact that he did more for them than anyone else, even her own family.

But then he didn't have a choice. If it hadn't been for him, she would still have a loving husband to take care of her.

As if she could read his mind, Maria said softly, "When are you going to stop blaming yourself for Tim's death?"

"Never," Matt said flatly.

"It was an accident. You have got to come to grips with that."

Despite her brave words, Matt heard the tremor in her voice, and he damned himself for calling her in the first place. The last thing he needed was more guilt.

"Don't worry about us, we're fine," Maria said.

"I do worry. You know that."

"You should be worrying about yourself."

"I am," he responded with dark humor.

"Haven't heard anything, huh?"

"I won't until those s.o.b.s get good and ready."

"Surely that woman insurance adjuster saw how desperately you needed a settlement."

"Look, Maria, I gotta go now. I'll be by to see you and Skipper soon, okay?"

"All . . . right," she said, as if taken aback by his abruptness.

"Give Skipper my love."

Matt placed the receiver in its cradle. He stared at it for a long minute, but he wasn't seeing it. Brittany's face swam before his eyes.

"Damn," he muttered, jumping up as if he'd been shot out of a cannon.

Sam's ears perked up, and he whined.

Matt stormed out the living room and into the kitchen where he grabbed a beer out of the refrigerator. Moments later, he stared at an empty bottle and didn't feel a bit better.

Maybe a cup of coffee was what he needed. No. That would just keep him awake, and lord knows he didn't need that. What he needed was a check so that he could replace his equipment and get into full operation. But more than that, he needed *not* to think about Brittany.

Not now. Not ever.

He laughed a bitter laugh. Too late, Diamond. He should've thought of that before he backed her up against the wall and made love to her until they were both limp and trembling.

To make matters worse, he hadn't left it there. He'd taken her to bed and tasted every delectable part of her body until her secrets were no longer hers alone, but his, as well.

The ache in his head that started earlier switched from one drum to a full ensemble.

"Come on, Sam," he said, "let's get the hell outside."

The warm night air was a balm to his battered senses. He stood on the porch and stared at the sky; the stars winked at him. Behind him a cricket chirped. Sam left his side and went to investigate; the hound sniffed the grass.

Matt scarcely paid him any attention. His thoughts were again on Brittany and on the uncomfortable swell in his jeans. He had to forget her; that was all there was to it. Their coming together was one of those crazy one-night stands, pure and simple. Ships passing in the night. Her disappearing act had shown him that.

And the Harvard dude in the three-piece suit who had shown up several days later further convinced him of that.

Forget her, he told himself. She wasn't worth it.

The porch swing groaned as he sat in it. He moved it in a lulling motion.

He didn't presume to know what made him lose his head that way. He could honestly say that none of the other women he'd known had ever affected him like that, made his blood boil to the extent that nothing else mattered.

Even now, he couldn't block out the little sounds she'd made when she reached a climax . . .

His insides were hot like a furnace about to blow. Shame and anger fought it out. Shame at his lust, anger that he couldn't control it. It built inside him, pressed against his groin.

He lunged out of the swing and jammed his hands into the pockets of his cutoff jeans. Anger was a better emotion to focus on right now. Letting her get to him was not only insane but counterproductive. What would be the point, anyway?

He would never see her again.

Eleven

Matt's jaw slackened, and he blinked several times. "Well, well, well. So you decided to come back to Hicksville after all."

Brittany's heart flipped at the sight of him. "Do you...mind if I come in?"

"Why would I?" he said, shifting his weight so that she could pass him.

He closed the door and followed her into the living room. The silence was oppressive. Still, she forced herself to face him.

But he didn't look at her; his head was turned toward the window filled with weak sunlight. She knew he was stunned; she'd seen it in his face when he'd opened the door. But she'd seen something else, as well, only she couldn't put a name to it. It didn't matter, though. She was a woman on a mission, and nothing before or after mattered. But everything in the middle was a source of pain.

She couldn't stop staring at him, though his profile offered little encouragement. His rough-hewn features wore a cold and forbidding expression. It was as if he hated her—this man who'd made love to her so wildly, so desperately, so completely, only a month ago.

"Did I catch you at a bad time?" The words were barely audible.

They studied each other for a long, smothering moment. Then Matt hooked a finger around a belt loop and leaned against the wall. "No. I just got home and out of the shower."

That was obvious, Brittany thought. Her eyes swept over his hair; drops of moisture clung to the tips like drops of dew. But she didn't stop there. Her gaze continued down to his tanned, shirtless chest, to the faded, ragged cutoffs that molded his thighs. My, but he looked good....

He seemed to have read her thoughts—his eyes shrunk to pinpoints, and his breathing turned harsh. And for another long moment, their eyes met.

"You want a cup of coffee?" he asked suddenly, as if desperate to dispel the tension.

Brittany knew she shouldn't. This wasn't a social call, far from it. The thought was so ludicrous that she would've laughed if she hadn't been afraid the laughter would quickly turn to tears. As it was, she'd cried enough the last few days to last her a lifetime.

"Please, just a half cup."

When he handed her the mug, their fingers inadvertently brushed. She felt a jolt. Her glance locked with his a second time. The memory of the way his hands and mouth had loved her was vivid. She remembered the violent harmony of their lovemaking, and the deep emotions that had overwhelmed her—emotions that she feared could be labeled love.

Something hard flickered over his features. "Why did you come back?"

Brittany couldn't answer. Her pulse throbbed in her ears, so much so that when she raised the cup to her lips, her hands shook.

He watched her, his eyelids at half-mast. "I'm waiting."

His tone was even, as though he was unaffected. She knew better. She heard the scraping sound underneath, like two pieces of sandpaper rubbing against each other. Sweat glistened on his forehead.

"I...we need to talk," she said, tightening her grip on her cup.

"You want to sit down?"

Although she felt as if there was nothing substantial beneath her feet, Brittany still couldn't sit down. What she had to say was best said from an upright position.

"I hope you came to settle, then, that you have a check in your purse."

She cast a wild look around the room. "No."

"No?"

"No."

His brows formed a scowl, making him appear more threatening than ever. "Then just why the hell *are* you here?"

Brittany felt as if a hard object poked her in the ribs and made speech impossible.

"What you did was wrong, you know," he said unexpectedly, "running out without saying anything."

His face had a curiously vulnerable look to it. She turned away, numb and slightly sick. "I know."

"Then why did you?"

Reluctantly she faced him again. "I...I was afraid."

"Of me?"

Her breath came out a tight whisper. "No, of myself."

The seconds ticked away.

"Brittany..." His voice sounded hoarse suddenly, as though he had a terrible cold. He took a step toward her.

She backed away. "No...don't...please."

As if he remembered the last time she had said similar words to him, his eyes sparked, and tension stiffened his jaw. He seemed in danger of exploding.

"Matt...I..."

"What's going on, Brittany?"

She set her mug down and hugged slick hands to her sides. "I have something to tell you."

"Ah, so that's it. The decision's been made. I'm going to get screwed out of my—"

She gave her head a violent shake. "No!"

"Then what? You're not making sense."

There was a long pause.

"I...I didn't come here to talk about the claim."

His eyes were so direct, so piercing, that her nerve slipped. But only for a second. She came here to play the hand that had been dealt her, no matter what.

"Dammit! If you don't hurry up..."

"I'm pregnant, Matt."

Shock stripped his face of expression.

Brittany's heart hurt. She was certain it had cracked open and was oozing the pain.

"You're what!"

She drew in a quick, hollow breath. Oh, God, she thought. His words, his tone wounded her like a low blow. Her worst fears were reality. She hadn't known for sure how he would react, but she had imagined this scenario. She should have been prepared.

Only she wasn't. And it hurt. It hurt so badly that she felt battered inside and out.

Still—it had taken two. He had enjoyed their romp in the bed as much as she had. They both should be hanged, first for ever letting it happen, and second, for not taking precautions.

Stupid! Stupid! Stupid! That was what she had said to herself when the doctor told her that she was pregnant. Not only had she condemned herself, but she'd panicked.

So why should she be so disappointed in Matt's reaction?

Perhaps it was because he was staring at her as if she wasn't there. Only she was, and he had heard her, heard every word she'd said.

"I'm going to have a baby," she repeated softly. *"Your baby."*

Their eyes met and held.

Time slowed to a crawl. Each second extended itself a hundredfold.

"I..." His lips snapped together as if it was impossible to say a word.

"I thought you had a right to know," she whispered, trembling inside. "That's why I told you. But I don't expect anything from you."

His eyes narrowed to slits. "Exactly what does that mean?"

This was worse then her wildest imagination. He stood in front of her like a solid block of ice, totally and completely unapproachable.

"It means that I intend to take care of the child since an abortion—"

"An abortion!" His face turned purple with rage. "Never! You hear!"

Brittany placed her hands over her ears. "Stop it!"

He swore.

"You didn't let me finish."

"So finish."

"I never even considered getting rid of the...baby."

"And why not? I can't imagine you wanting a child."

She felt as if she was being strangled. Her eyes filled with tears. "I didn't realize how much you hated me."

"I don't hate you." His voice sounded as though he'd swallowed glass. "It would be simpler if I did, though."

A silence stretched.

"Are you sure you're pregnant?"

"Yes."

"There's no possible room for error?"

"Do you want to see the doctor's report?"

"No."

Another silence.

"Look, this conversation is going nowhere, so I'll be going...."

He reached out and circled her forearm. "I don't think so."

Brittany stared at his hand, then looked at him, all the while praying she wouldn't burst into tears. They were perilously close. "Excuse me?"

"You're not going anywhere until this is settled."

She pulled away and eased toward the door. She couldn't take much more. She felt herself sliding out of control. She had to get out of there before she made a complete fool of herself.

"As far as I'm concerned, it is settled."

"Like hell! If you *are* pregnant, no child of mine is going to be born a bastard."

"So what do you suggest, then?"

Her quietly spoken words fell into the silence like a chunk of lead.

"I suggest we get married, that's what."

Her heart jerked. "Do you... do you know what you're saying?"

"Yes. Will you marry me?"

Paralysis invaded Brittany's body. She couldn't move. She couldn't speak. Nor could she think. Only she had to. Most people at one time or other were forced to make a momentous decision. Now was her time. Sometimes you were prepared. Most of the time you weren't. It came without warning, and once answered, nothing would be ever the same again.

The question hung in the air like tempting but forbidden fruit. Brittany realized that in her heart of hearts, she'd wanted him to say that. But she didn't kid herself that just because he wanted to marry her, everything was going to be wonderful.

Matt was a stranger to her. Nevertheless, she loved him. She'd known that the minute he'd opened the door today. Insane or not, she'd fallen in love. But she wouldn't be blinded by that love. She would, though, for the sake of the child she carried inside her, make the marriage work.

"Brittany..." Matt's voice cracked.

She swallowed the tightness in her throat. "What?"

"Come here."

With a cry, she ran into his arms. He held her close to his heart.

Finally, she pulled back and stared at him. "What now?"

He kissed her on the tip of the nose. It was a spontaneous gesture, she knew, which made it all the more special.

"Set a date," he said thickly.

Her smile was wobbly. "You're right."

"When do you want to...do it?"

"When do you?"

"Soon."

"How soon?"

"Two, maybe three days at the latest." His gaze probed hers. "We have to think about the baby, you know."

Brittany placed her hand on her still flat stomach and smiled as heat filled her cheeks. Now that she'd consented to marry him, she was shaken, as though she'd awakened from an unreal dream. "That's fine."

"What about your daddy?"

Her face crumpled. Then she recovered. "I'll have to tell him, of course."

"The sooner the better, I would imagine." Matt cleared his throat. "Do you want me to go with you?"

"No...no. I think it'd be best if I told him myself."

"Fine by me."

She smiled a small smile. "We...we have so much to talk about."

"I know."

"When will I see you again?"

"Tomorrow, of course," he said, before kissing her on the mouth, a hot, searing kiss. Then he pushed her back to arm's length. "I don't want to get something started..."

Brittany flushed. "It's all right to touch me, you know. I'm pregnant, not sick."

"The only problem is that if you don't go now, you won't go at all."

Her heart turned over under his smoldering grin. "Er...right. I'll see you tomorrow."

"Tomorrow," he echoed softly.

Marriage?

Impossible. Yesterday that word hadn't been in his vocabulary, much less on the agenda. It was on the agenda now, and he might as well get used to it.

A baby?

That was an equal impossibility. But one he had to face, as well.

Was he crazy to marry her? Yes. They were as different as two people could ever be. They had nothing in common, except a wild craving for each other. Love, thank God, didn't enter into it. Furthermore, he could never allow himself to fall in love with her. That would finish him.

But was the baby enough? And sex? Were those two things strong enough to hold them together? He took a deep breath. He felt dizzy, alarmingly light-headed and out of control.

He had no idea what time it was, nor did he care. He figured around three o'clock in the morning. After Brittany had left he'd gone to the shop, retrieved his toolbox and carburetor.

But he'd gotten little done. He hadn't been able to keep his mind on his job.

"Ouch!" he muttered, and jerked his hand away from the piece of equipment that sat on an old blanket on the floor in front of him.

He grabbed a rag out of his back pocket and wiped off his hand. Not much damage done, he noted, just a gash in his index finger. He wiped it again, and when it wouldn't stop bleeding, he decided to call it quits. For a minute he watched his hand shake. He knew where this lack of control stemmed from.

He stood and grunted loudly. His back felt as though it was broken in several places.

Sam whined, then licked Matt's other hand. Matt walked around for a bit, Sam in tow, then poured himself another cup of coffee and eased down in his chair. He wanted to sleep, but he knew if he closed his eyes, his mind wouldn't go blank.

He was still trying to come to grips with the hundred-degree turn his life had taken. Even now, he could feel his reaction when he'd opened the door and Brittany had stood on the steps. He'd felt gut-punched.

Yet he hadn't been able to move or take his eyes off her. Except for the tired look around her eyes, he'd never seen her look lovelier. The lime-green jumpsuit hinted at her voluptuous curves underneath, curves that could drive a man mad.

He ought to know. He'd felt that way until he'd touched, kissed, licked every square inch of that flesh. It had been paradise, all right. Only now he was about to pay for it—with his freedom.

But something else called him, something he'd never expected. Something frightening. But something equally as sweet.

"Sam, my boy, it won't be long till you hear the pitter-patter of little feet."

First, though, he had a marriage to attend. His own.

Twelve

Matt's head lay inside the curve of her arm. Shifting ever so slightly, he cupped the underside of her breast and lifted it to his lips.

Brittany sank her free hand into his hair, and her eyelids fluttered at the gentle tug on her nipple. Her thighs parted. He touched her there, and she heard him moan at her wetness.

Matt left his hand gloved around her warmth, then laved her breasts until her nipples were raw. Breathing became impossible, such was the heat that threatened to explode within her.

Eager to bring him the same sweet pain, Brittany surrounded him with her fingers and stroked. He moaned again and began to move his hand, which was still between her thighs.

"Oh, yes, Matt. Oh!"

Both sensed when the other had had enough. They changed positions and came together. He uttered words that made no sense as he slid all the way up her. The velvet contact seemed to go on forever, expanding to her stomach, her throat. Her mind melted. Her thighs quivered. Her breasts shook with wrenching emotion. Her very breath was dug out of her so that her heart pounded against him.

"I can't—wait," he whispered brokenly. "I'm sorry..."

His head moved, and his lips opened around a nipple. Hot. So hot. She burned as he eased his hand behind her, to her buttocks, and lifted her.

He was everywhere inside her. He used his body to render her mindless. His gasp mingled with her moan as she clutched him to her. She loved the way he felt, his body wedged between her thighs.

Her climax snuck up on her. She pressed her face into the muscles of his shoulder, tasted the salt and scent of him at the exact moment her inner muscles trapped him tightly within. She felt only the beginnings of his explosion when simultaneously they cried out and he spilled into her.

They continued to hold each other, then fell into a deep, dreamless sleep.

Brittany woke, stretched, then glanced at Matt, who was still asleep. A smile broke across her lips, and for a moment she was content to watch him, thinking about the way he'd made love to her. No matter how or when he touched her, he had the power to turn her inside out. To touch him was like touching a live wire, almost too intense to bear. Yet she couldn't seem to get enough of him, nor he of her.

Sometimes, though, she had to pinch herself to make sure this was real, that she and Matt had actually been married two months. But what was more mystifying was that they were happy, which was not to say there hadn't been disagreements—there had.

At first, there was the awkwardness of two people living together who hadn't been privy to each other's bad habits and idiosyncrasies. Each day had been a learning experience.

Both had volatile personalities, and both were independent. Consequently, they had to learn to give and take.

The most serious disagreement had come a week after they'd married. Matt had come in from the woods early to shower and shave before they left for a barbecue at a fellow logger's house.

They had been dressing when she turned to Matt and asked, "Are you happy with your work?"

Matt stopped what he was doing and stared at her with an incredulous expression on his face. "What the hell kind of question is that?"

"You know we've never really talked about our future," Brittany responded hesitantly, realizing she was treading on dangerous ground.

"What does that have to do with my work?"

"I think that would be obvious."

"Not to me," he said flatly.

"You wouldn't consider doing something else, then, something less dangerous?"

"Like what?" His tone told her he was not happy in the least with the conversation.

"Oh, I don't know." Her eyes pleaded. "It's just that we have a child to think about now…" Her voice played out.

His eyes dulled. "You don't like living here."

"Excuse me?"

"That's what this is all about, isn't it? It's not so much my work but where *you* have to live."

"I never said that," she retorted.

"No, that's right, you didn't. But you didn't have to."

Tears welled in her eyes, and she held out a hand to him. "Matt…please…don't be mad at me."

His eyes were tortured. "Oh, God, Brittany, why I let you twist me in knots, I'll never know."

"Kiss me," she demanded, sliding her tongue wetly along her bottom lip.

He groaned and reached for her. They never made it to the barbecue.

That one incident had taught them both how thin-skinned they were and how much work was ahead of them.

All in all, though, the change in Matt had been quite remarkable. He was no longer the tense, angry loner he'd been when she'd met him. He seemed to genuinely enjoy being married, especially the time they spent in bed.

If there was a murky cloud on the otherwise clear horizon, it was her daddy. But then she couldn't blame Walter entirely for his attitude. She had stuck to her decision not to confide in him until after she and Matt were married.

This decision was not without its consequences. She grieved that Walter hadn't been included in such a momentous event in her life. She loved him, and he should have been there to give her away.

Short of locking her up, he could have done nothing to stop the wedding. But she had wanted to avoid his cold disapproval.

Only after they married in a private ceremony in Nacogdoches did Brittany drive to Tyler without Matt and tell Walter.

"Have you lost your mind?" he'd yelled, his face growing redder by the second.

"No, Daddy, far from it."

"But...why, for god's sake? Surely you don't think it'll last." He rubbed his forehead vigorously as though he had a dilly of a headache. "He's nothing but a damn redneck!"

"Daddy—"

"Don't you daddy me! What are you trying to do? Make me the laughingstock of my own company?"

"That's...a horrible thing to say." Waves of disgust crashed through her.

Walter turned away, then whirled. "I can pull some strings and have it annulled, you know."

"I'm pregnant, Daddy."

He stared at her dumbfounded. He opened his mouth, only to shut it with a snap.

Her eyes closed briefly in pain. "Matt insisted we get married, and I said okay."

Walter turned pale, then said coldly, "Something you'll live to regret, I assure you."

Brittany reached out a hand. "Daddy, please . . . try to be glad, if not about my marriage, then about the baby." She paused and drew air through her lungs. "You've always wanted a grandchild."

"But not Matthew Diamond's. By god, have you forgotten that he's under suspicion for sabotaging his own equipment?"

"Matt says he's innocent, and I believe him."

Walter smirked. "Well, I can see he sold you a bill of goods."

"I know I probably didn't handle this right, but I knew you wouldn't approve." She rubbed the back of her neck wearily. "I . . . I wanted my baby to have a name."

Walter's expression remained grim. "Howard would've married you."

"Oh, Daddy, how can you say that?" Her voice broke. "Anyway, that wouldn't have been fair to him. He deserves better."

"When do I get to meet your . . . hus—Matt?"

Brittany thought he might choke on the words. She sighed a heartfelt sigh. "Soon, I promise."

"So I take it you're going to live in the woods."

"Right."

"Have you thought about the child growing up in that environment?" Walter shook his head. "I just hope you know what you're doing."

"I do." Brittany's voice almost faltered, but didn't. Not for one second would she let him know that she'd had the same reservations.

"What about your work?"

"Nothing's changed there. I'll just use Lufkin as my base."

"I don't like it. I don't like it one damn bit."

"I'm happy, Daddy. Everthing's going to be all right, you'll see." She leaned over and kissed his cool cheek, fully expecting him to flinch. Surprisingly, he didn't. "I have to go now."

Following that conversation, she'd faced Howard. Like Walter, he had told her outright that she had married beneath herself, that Matt was not the man for her and that it would never last. She had told him she was sorry he felt that way and left it at that.

While neither of those encounters had been pleasant, she hadn't let them damper her resolve to make a success of her marriage, for her baby's sake if nothing else.

Still, she wished her daddy had reacted differently. She had thought the baby would have turned him around. Would she ever please him? More to the point, would she ever stop trying? She doubted it, and that was what scared her the most.

"When am I going to feel the baby move?"

Matt's voice jarred her back to the moment. He was awake now, and was massaging her stomach. She smiled and covered his hand with hers. "Any day, the doctor says."

"What were you thinking about just now?"

"Daddy," she said honestly.

"Think he'll ever come around?"

"Maybe, maybe not."

Matt inhaled deeply. "No regrets?"

"None." She shifted positions so as to look him in the eye. "How about you?"

"Same here."

"Truthfully, I had my doubts."

"Me, too," he said with a grin. "Because you're such a spoiled brat."

She punched him in the ribs. "That remark is going to cost you, buddy."

"I'm easy."

She smiled. "Don't I know that."

"Are you complaining?" His breath tickled her skin.

"No," she whispered.

They were quiet for a moment, content to hold each other close and listen to the crickets chirp outside the window.

"What time is it?" Matt finally asked.

"Does it matter?"

"No, except I figure it's about time for me to haul my buns out of bed."

"It's still dark."

"Good."

"Bruce called."

Matt's grin faded. "And?"

"A decision hasn't been made yet, I'm afraid."

Matt opened his mouth to say something, then closed it. Since they had been married, he had never asked her whether she thought him innocent or guilty. Because it was such a delicate subject, they had skirted the issue. The case was still under investigation, and he hadn't gotten his money.

To pay his heavy equipment bill, Matt had rented a friend's skidder and loader. The mill in Lufkin was buying all the pulpwood he could deliver. Consequently, he put in long hours. And that meant Brittany was alone a lot. But she had her own work to keep her occupied, and she was busy making plans for the baby.

"Mind if we don't talk business?" he said. His lips explored the hollow at her throat. "Mm, you smell delicious."

"I do?"

Matt propped himself up on an elbow and smiled at her. The moon that flooded the room allowed her to see his eyes. They seemed bottomless, and blue like the ocean. The fringe of lashes was black against his tanned skin. "Why do men always have the thickest lashes? It's not fair."

"Huh? Who told you life was fair?" He leaned his forehead against hers. "Maybe our son will be so endowed."

"Daughter."

"Oh, you think so?"

Brittany raised her head and nipped his ear. "I know so."

"We'll see," he said, then kissed her and placed a leg over hers.

She felt his hardness against her stomach. "I thought you said you had to go to work?"

"So, I lied."

Brittany was positive the tree touched heaven. She leaned her head back to see the top. She couldn't. Only after she felt the strain on her neck and found she couldn't swallow did she lower her head. For a moment the world spun.

She took a deep breath and balanced herself against the nearest tree. The world quickly righted itself, and she looked at her surroundings.

A safe distance from her, Matt's crew worked. This was the first time she'd been to the woods to see his operation. Matt had waited until the weather was perfect—less heat and low humidity—then had insisted she come with him. She suspected it was to prove that if he was careful, his work was no more dangerous than anyone else's.

She didn't argue, although she despised the thought of encountering snakes and bugs.

"Are . . . there snakes?" she'd asked hesitantly.

He'd laughed out loud. "Snakes. Why, of course not. Where did you get that idea?"

She didn't think his teasing was one bit funny. She kept one eye on his men and the other on the ground.

The borrowed skidder dragged a tree that had just been cut to the set—Matt had explained that the set was the working area around the pile of logs.

Two men with chain saws waited to cut the logs so that the loader could pick them up and transport them to the trucks. She found the job fascinating, especially when they felled a tree, something they were about to do now.

Brittany's eyes scanned the premise around the huge pine, certain she would find the saw in Matt's hand. About that time he sauntered up to the base of the tree. He paused and flashed her a crooked grin.

Her stomach flip-flopped. Even dirty and in dire need of a shave, he looked sexy as hell, she thought, watching as he placed the saw against the truck and began to move it. The muscles in his shoulders and biceps bunched while sweat broke out on his face.

It wasn't until the task was nearly done that she took her eyes off Matt and looked up. The tree, as if in slow motion, began falling toward the ground.

Halfway there, someone yelled, *"Timber!"*

The sound was deafening as the huge tree struck the ground. Her heart climbed in her throat. Brittany shuddered to think what would happen if a tree turned the wrong way. She'd had no idea of the danger Matt faced every day. No wonder the casualty count among loggers was so high, not to mention their insurance rates.

But she didn't have time to dwell on that thought. Matt waved at her, and she relaxed.

He held the thumbs-up sign.

The hour that followed proved to be anticlimactic. She leaned against the tree and watched as the men worked.

"Gotcha."

A hand flew to her chest. Strong arms embraced her from behind.

She twisted her head. "Matthew Diamond, you nearly scared me out of ten years' growth. Besides, you're wet," she added primly.

He nuzzled her neck. "Wanna take a shower with me when we get home?"

"I'll think about it."

"How's my boy?" His hand fell to her stomach.

"I think I felt *her* move this morning, but I'm not sure."

"Mm, I'll have to check that out in the shower."

"I don't need a shower."

"Wanna bet?"

She slapped him playfully on the neck. "You have a one-track mind."

"You're a fine one to be talking." He patted her on the butt. "Come on, woman, let's go home."

Brittany didn't know what woke her. Was it the burning in her chest? Or was it the niggling pain in her lower stomach? She rolled over, careful not to disturb Matt.

She lay on her side and stared out the window into the darkness. She tried to find the stars, but as far as she could tell, there was none.

Why hadn't she listened to Matt and eaten only one piece of pizza instead of two? But they had been celebrating her fourth month of pregnancy and the movement of the baby for the first time.

She eased up and sat on the side of the bed. The tiny pain kept on coming. Finally, she got up and padded into the bathroom.

A few minutes later, she started crying.

She heard his feet hit the floor. Within seconds he stood inside the bathroom door.

"Oh, God, Matt," she sobbed.

He knelt in front of her and took her cold, clammy hands in his. "What's wrong, baby?" Panic weakened his voice.

"Help me, please." She clutched her stomach and bent over.

"Tell me what's wrong! Where do you hurt?"

Tears drenched her face. "Oh, God," Brittany said again. "I'm bleeding, Matt, I'm bleeding."

Thirteen

―――

"**I**'m sorry, Mrs. Diamond, but you lost the baby."

Those words. Those piercing, hurtful words. It had been six weeks since the doctor had come into the emergency room at the hospital and told her about the baby. And now, the words struck her again as if someone had put a fist into her stomach.

She couldn't make any sound but a soft, pitiful moan. She felt as if a piece of her own flesh had been ripped from her. It had.

She had only carried the tiny life inside her a short time, but she had wanted this baby so much—an emotion she had thought she'd never feel. But that was before Matt, before she fell in love.

She had pictured this baby in her mind as looking exactly like Matt, especially if it had been a boy.

Ah, Matt. The loss of the baby had hit him hard, as well. Yet they seemed unable to comfort each other.

He had withdrawn. After he'd come in from the woods, long periods of silence would follow. He almost never smiled. Their binding thread was the baby. They were more like strangers than ever before, except in the bed. They couldn't communicate with words, but they had no trouble with their bodies. Their lovemaking was more intense, as if it bordered on desperation.

Still, Brittany sensed that Matt felt trapped, that he'd only married her because it had been the right thing to do.

Work became her panacea for heartache. She pushed herself harder, begging for as many claim settlements as Wade would give her. She traveled to Tyler at least once a week, sometimes twice. But never far from her thoughts was the baby she had lost.

Today was no exception. She had driven until the tears made it impossible to see. Now, after getting out of the car and walking through a wooded area, she eased down at the foot of a tree and waited for the pain to subside.

It never did.

Sweat oozed out of every pore on Matt's body. It ran so heavily down his face that even his sweatband failed to stop it. Maybe that was because the band was drenched, he reminded himself as he kept on running.

He hadn't gone to the woods this morning. It had rained all day yesterday, and he couldn't take a chance on getting his equipment stuck in the mud. Consequently, he had too much time on his hands to think.

Losing his child was a scenario he had never foreseen, something beyond his worst nightmares. Yet he knew life had to go on, *must* go on.

Brittany didn't feel the same, and that was a shame. He'd tried to be patient, but she had closed him out. Maybe that was his fault, he'd been filled with such deep despair that he couldn't reach out to her.

He'd never been good at that sort of thing. He guessed he'd always been too much of a loner.

Now the gulf between them was widening, and Matt feared he was going to lose her, which was something he couldn't bear to think about, much less let happen.

By the time he turned into the drive leading to his workshop, he'd run five miles. He was exhausted. His mental capabilities weren't so far gone, however, that he failed to notice the door to his shop was ajar. When he left, it hadn't been that way.

"Son of a bitch!" Matt muttered, racing toward it. But when he got inside, no one was there. They had been, though. He couldn't tell right off if anything was missing, but he knew someone had been there. And he'd bet things were missing.

Just what the hell was going on? Breaking and entering was the final straw.

"You can have another baby, you know."

Brittany turned and faced her husband. She knew he was there; out of the corner of one eye, she had seen him drive up and park.

His voice was soft, but drained.

Her eyes met his, and there was desperation in them. "I know...that's what the doctor said."

"Will you, then?"

"Another baby won't take the place of this one."

A muscle jerked in his jaw. "I never said it would."

"Then what are you saying?"

"I'm saying I want us to...to try again, to have another baby."

Brittany's head felt heavy, as if she'd slept too long and too hard. She couldn't think. "I'm not sure that's possible. Anyway, it's...it's too soon." Her voice broke.

"Brittany, you've got to get hold of yourself."

"It's...easy for you—"

"It was my baby, too." He swallowed over and over.

"I know, and I'm sorry." She was, too, sorry for herself and sorry for him. She didn't mean to hurt him, but she couldn't seem to stop.

Matt took a harsh, deep breath. "Look, I have to go over to Maria's and take care of something for her." He paused. "You wanna come?"

"Yes. I'd like that."

His grave expression turned to surprise, and he blinked. That was when she saw the tears. One trickled down his cheek into his mouth.

"Maria, thanks for the coffee and cake." Brittany smiled. "Both were delicious."

Maria's face glowed. "I baked the cake for Matt as I always do—when I know he's coming, that is." Maria's dark eyes widened. "I hope you don't mind.

I mean, we owe Matt so much, I could never begin to repay him."

"Of course I don't mind," Brittany responded warmly. "He thinks the world of you, too."

She smiled again in hopes of putting the woman at ease. Maria Frost was not a pretty woman. She was downright mousy looking, with limp brown hair and eyes. But when she smiled her sweet smile, a person instantly began to rethink his assessment of her. Her smile made her beautiful.

Most of all, she was a good mother. Her three-year-old son was adorable. While Matt had taken care of several chores for Maria, Brittany had played with the baby. Later Matt had joined the two of them on the floor. She'd been astounded at Matt's patience with the child. When he'd read Skipper a book, she'd had to leave, imagining him doing that with their own child. The pain had almost crushed her. Matt had known it, too; his troubled eyes had followed her out of the room.

Maria had made her feel better, telling her some of the antics that Matt and Tim had pulled. Brittany had laughed.

Now, as the two of them stood beside the truck, waiting for Matt to join her so that they could leave, Brittany held out her hand. "I hope you'll come see me soon."

Maria frowned. "I'm such a homebody, I don't know."

"Well, at least think about it. If you don't come see me, I'll just have to come back and see you."

Maria looked beyond Brittany's shoulder suddenly and waved. Brittany twisted her neck. Heading toward them was a young man who looked to be in his late teens or early twenties. He had longish, unkempt brown hair and sullen features. Brittany disliked him on the spot.

"That's Billy, Tim's brother. I want him to meet you."

"Hi, Sis," Billy said, lumbering up to his sister-in-law's side.

"Billy, this is Matt's wife, Brittany."

"Mrs. Diamond."

"Hello, Billy," she said politely, thinking how his eyes shifted in his thin face, and he never quite looked at her.

Suddenly an arm came around her neck. Brittany peered into her husband's face. He stared at her. "I see you've met Billy."

"Uh-huh."

"Matt, thanks again for all you've done this afternoon," Maria put in quietly.

"Ah, it's nothing. Only I don't know how much longer you can put off getting the house reshingled."

Maria's face fell. "Oh, Matt you know I can't afford—"

"Don't say that. Don't even think it. As long as I'm here, you can afford anything you need."

An uncomfortable silence descended over the clear summer afternoon. Then Billy laughed a humorless laugh. "Huh—that's for sure. He hasn't got work for me these last few months—got no money. But you heard the man, Sis. Anything you want, you can have.''

''Be quiet, Billy,'' she said tersely.

He shrugged and turned away.

Goodbyes were said, and Brittany and Matt headed down the drive in his pickup.

''Maria's a nice lady,'' she said, filling the long silence. ''I like her a lot.'' Brittany paused and cleared her throat. ''And her little boy is precious.''

''Ours will be, too, you wait and see.''

His tone was so tender that for a moment Brittany couldn't speak. She cleared her throat and was finally able to get the words out before they choked her. ''About another baby—''

''We don't have to discuss it right now,'' Matt interrupted. The tenderness was still there, but so was something else—rough desperation. ''I agree. It's too early. We'll just give that subject a rest for a while. Okay?''

''Okay,'' she murmured weakly.

The silence turned almost deafening.

''When Tim died, why didn't Maria sue?'' Brittany asked. She couldn't stand the quiet another minute.

Matt's sigh was long and deep. ''Actually, I told her she had every right to.''

''She would have gotten a lot more money, that's for sure.''

''Money's not everything.''

Brittany ignored the barb. ''It's because she cares so much about you that she didn't sue.''

"Probably. Tim and I were the best of friends. He was several years older than Maria, and he thought the sun rose and set on her."

"Maria seemed devoted to him, too."

"She worshiped him. He took her out of an abusive home situation. But then Billy worshiped him, too." He suddenly pounded the wheel with his right hand. "If only Tim had listened to me that day when I warned him about the skidder."

Matt's face and voice were those of a demented man. She laid one hand on his arm, offering what comfort she could. "I would feel the same way."

"She makes a mean cake, doesn't she?" he asked, seemingly back in control.

Brittany shifted her head to one side. "That she does. But do I detect another meaning in that statement?"

He laughed, one of his rare belly laughs, then looked at her. "Have I ever criticized your cooking?"

"No, but you don't compliment it, either."

"Well . . . let's just say your expertise doesn't lie in the kitchen." He grinned. "And no pun intended."

"Funny."

He reached over and squeezed her fingers. "Trust me, between the two of us, we won't starve."

Brittany watched as he removed his hand and placed it around the steering wheel. Such strong, capable hands, she thought. Hands that could set her bare flesh on fire. She flushed, but still she didn't remove her eyes.

They were on the open highway. He seemed to take great pleasure in handling the truck at a speed that attested to his other skills and ability. The road claimed all his attention. It was almost as if she weren't with him.

Dangerous. That was the word that suddenly came to mind. He looked dangerous—flint-eyed and silent. When he was in this mood, she could see the hard streak in him. She wasn't frightened; instead it intrigued her.

How did he feel about her? Did he love her? Did he think the sun rose and set on her? Or did he just *want* her? She didn't know. She honestly didn't know.

One thing she was sure of—Matt wasn't capable of sabotaging his own equipment. She was more convinced now than when she'd defended him to her daddy. It wasn't his style. Granted, he was obstinate and proud to a fault, but he was no thief. Had she not already known that down deep, the trip to Maria's would have proved it. Besides, he loved what he did too much to jeopardize losing it all.

If he wasn't the guilty one, then who was? Brittany was convinced that foul play was involved, that his troubles weren't bad luck.

She had a gut feeling who the culprit might be.

She faced Matt again, only this time her thoughts pertained to business. "He hates you, you know."

Matt cut his eyes toward her. "Who?"

"Billy."

"What makes you say that?"

"I saw the way he looked at you. Hate definitely shone from his eyes."

"I guess he has reason to," Matt said bleakly.

"You know better than that." Her tone was sharp. "It was an accident. Maria certainly doesn't hold you responsible. Why should his brother?"

"Beats me. If there is an explanation, it's that he was so close to Tim, relied on him for everything."

Brittany shivered. "There's something about him that makes me uneasy, that makes my skin crawl, actually. I don't trust him."

"That's interesting," Matt mused, searching her face before turning back to the road. "That's very interesting, indeed."

"Matt?"

"Mm?"

"I told them I changed my mind, that your claim was legit and to let it go through."

Matt slowed down abruptly and stared at her, and though his eyes were warm, he only said, "Thanks."

They finished the trip in silence, only to have that silence turn even more awkward when they stood in the middle of the living room a short time later and faced each other.

An unguarded flicker of passion passed between them.

Matt lowered his eyes. "Uh, are you coming to bed?"

"Yes," she said softly, and reached for his hand.

Fourteen

The sky was streaked with color. The wind blew the trees just enough so that the sun peeped through and seared her skin.

Brittany didn't mind. She was already drenched with perspiration. This afternoon was the second time she had gone to the Livewell Fitness Club in Lufkin and worked out.

She remained in her car for a minute and listened to her heart pound. But the sound this time was a healthy one.

The trauma of the miscarriage had dulled somewhat, and she was making strides to get her life back on track. She had increased her work load and was out of town at least two or three days a week.

She had hoped that work, combined with physical exertion, would help fill the void inside her. Was she the only married woman who was lonely? Probably not. While Matt was considerate, polite and passionate as ever in bed, he continued to hold his emotions in check.

The wedge that her miscarriage had created was still there. And widening. She knew he cared about her, but that wasn't good enough. She wanted him to *love* her. Perhaps if she told him she loved him it would make a difference. Perhaps it wouldn't. Anyway, the words simply wouldn't come.

And then there was the problem of the upcoming meeting between Matt and her daddy. Walter insisted on meeting his son-in-law, and Brittany knew she couldn't put it off any longer. She didn't want her daddy to know there were problems in her marriage. She didn't want to hear him say, "I told you so," although he had been surprisingly comforting when she'd told him about the baby. She'd sensed that he was disappointed, and that warmed her heart.

Brittany paused in her thoughts to wipe the sweat out of her eyes. She glanced at her watch and saw that it was late. Matt would be home soon, and they planned to go to Annie's Padlock for dinner.

She reached for her gym bag and stepped out of the car. She was just starting toward the house when she saw a movement out of the corner of her eye. She thought she had imagined it, but she stopped and looked again. She knew she hadn't been mistaken.

Someone was in Matt's workshop. Who? And why? Elmer, she knew, was in the woods with Matt. Had he sent one of his other hands after something? No, that wasn't possible, because there would have been a car in the drive. It was empty.

A frown marred her brow, but she pushed aside the flutter of fear and marched toward the shop.

She didn't know what it was that kept her from charging up to the door. Instead, she crept to a front window and peered inside.

Brittany watched for a moment while the intruder walked the premises, picking up first one tool, then another as if taking inventory.

She crossed to the door. She had her hand on the knob when the door suddenly opened.

Billy Frost froze in his tracks. And the expression on his face was one of a cat caught with a canary between its teeth.

"Er...hello, Mrs. Diamond," he stammered, not looking at her.

"What are you doing here, Billy?" Brittany demanded, her tone direct and sharp.

"Er...well, you see—"

"No, I don't see. Suppose you tell me."

He fidgeted and stared into space.

"Billy!" Brittany's voice sharpened. She was hot and tired and desperately wanted a shower.

"I was looking for a tool to fix a faucet leak for Maria," he said quickly. Too quickly.

"Why aren't you working today?"

"Matt didn't need me," he said sullenly, drawing circles on the ground with the toe of a dirty tennis shoe.

"How did you get here?"

He moved his head toward the rear of the building. "My bicycle. I... I came the back way, through the woods."

Brittany pursed her lips. "Did it ever occur to you to ask permission to borrow something?"

"No one was home." His stance bordered on belligerent.

"Then you should've left." Brittany crossed her arms and leaned against a wall. "You know what I think, Billy?"

"No."

"I think you're lying."

His face flushed a deep, ugly red.

"Not for one minute do I think you were here to get a tool."

"I don't care what you think," he shot back, his eyes reminding her of those of a trapped animal.

Brittany shrugged. "The leaky faucet is easy enough to check out. In fact—"

His lightning-quick movement stuffed the words back down Brittany's throat. Before she could react, he darted past her and was out the door. She ran after him, but he was on his bicycle and peddling as if the very devil were after him.

"You little bone-headed jerk," Brittany muttered, thrusting her hands deep into her already disheveled hair.

"Hey!"

She spun and watched as Matt climbed out of his truck.

"Darn it," Brittany said, meeting him halfway.

Only after he grabbed her upper arms did she realize she was shaking.

"Was that Billy I saw tearing off through the woods?" A frown added to the tiredness of his face.

"One and the same," Brittany responded tightly.

Matt's frown intensified as he dropped his arms to his side. "What's going on?"

"I came home from the gym and caught him in the shop."

"Whatever for?"

"You tell me."

"You mean he didn't?"

Brittany's face was reddened with anger. "Oh, he gave me a paltry explanation. Said he was after a tool so he could fix a leak for Maria."

Matt grunted. "That'll be the day."

"That's what I thought. I bet he wouldn't know which end to screw on a faucet."

"And you would?"

She blinked. "Excuse me?"

"And you would," he repeated, a slow grin spreading across his lips.

Twin flags of color stained her cheeks. How dare he laugh at her? "I fail to see the humor in this," she said hotly.

"And I don't see why you're getting so upset."

"Oh, you don't? Well, I do." Her insides clenched while her voice rose. "Either you're ignoring what's right in front of your eyes or you're a bigger fool than I thought!"

The muscles in his cheeks bunched, and his eyes could have melted iron. "I'd watch what I was saying, if I were you."

She sensed his anger and backed up, but she didn't back down. "I think it's Billy who's behind your equipment troubles."

He laughed. "Billy? No way. He's worthless as hell. He doesn't have enough sense to get in out of a good hard rain, much less steal and damage equipment."

"Damn you, Matthew Diamond!"

The humor fled his face. "Why, you're serious, aren't you?"

"Yes."

He looked at her suddenly with an exhaustion that seemed to go all the way through him. "Got any proof?"

"No, other than my instinct, which says he was up to no good this afternoon. And he does hate you, which you already know. And he also blames you for Tim's death."

Something flickered in Matt's eyes. "All right, you win. I'll keep a closer eye on him, and we'll see."

"Good." Her voice had an edge to it. "Now that that's settled, I'm going to take a shower."

One side of his mouth tightened, and he didn't say anything.

Sudden fatigue tugged at her. She turned and took several steps, feeling his eyes bore into her back.

"Brittany?"

She stopped and turned.

His eyes met hers. "In case you didn't know it, you look great in those tights," he drawled. "In fact you've got the best looking butt I've ever seen."

She fought back a smile. He never ceased to surprise her. One minute his emotions ran hot, the next cold

She doubted she'd ever understand him.

"Want some company?"

The soap slipped out of her hand and hit the bottom of the shower with a loud impact.

"Sorry, I didn't mean to scare you."

"You didn't," Brittany whispered, not bothering to hide her body from his scrutiny.

She looked like a goddess under a waterfall, Matt thought, swallowing hard. The perfection of her slender neck, firm, tilted breasts, long legs couldn't have been captured on canvas no matter how masterful the artist.

When he realized that she wasn't saying anything, he saw her eyes raking over him, taking in his sunbaked skin, lean muscles crisscrossing his chest, shoulders, arms, and the taut trimness of his hips.

"Your body's beautiful," she said breathlessly.

Blood thundered through Matt and settled in his groin.

She reached out and circled its hardness and drew him toward her. In that moment, as the water splashed over him, he thought he might die.

"Brittany, Brittany," he groaned.

She leaned against the wall, out of the direct line of spray, her hand still wrapped around him like a hot glove.

"Tell me what you want." Her words came out a guttural cry.

He dropped to his knees, looked up and said, "I want you. All of you."

"I want that, too."

He found the bar of soap, lathered his hands and began to rub between each of her toes, the top of her foot, up the front and inside of her thigh.

When he reached the crisp red curls, he lingered for endless minutes.

"Oh, Matt!" Brittany cried. She thrust her hands into his hair and held him against her.

He journeyed upward until he stood, his mouth against her neck, her throat, her eyes and breasts, devouring her.

Brittany trapped him between her sudsy legs and began suddenly to move. He felt as though the top of his head was going to come off.

"Let's go to the bed," he whispered into her mouth. "I want you on top, to see your face."

Only when he was inside her, hot and throbbing, did he feel that she truly belonged to him. Even then, there were doubts. He lived in fear of returning home some evening and finding a note telling him that she'd left him, that she'd gone back to Tyler.

Still, he couldn't stop himself from longing for her, not just now, but constantly. Where she was concerned, he felt like he was on a long, turbulent roller coaster ride, one that he couldn't get off even when it was over.

"Make love to me," Brittany begged, her eyes glazed with passion.

Matt held her against him with one hand. The other he used to open the door. Carefully, he backed out of the shower, dragging her with him.

She chose that moment to tighten her hands on his buttocks.

"Oh, Brittany..."

They never made it to the bed.

Fifteen

"**W**hat do you think?"

Maria's plain features brightened, and she smiled. "Oh, Brittany, it's lovely."

Brittany looked concerned. "Lovely. Now that's a word I don't think Matt will—"

"Oh, I didn't mean it like that," Maria interrupted. "I guess what I meant to say was that it looks great."

Brittany's face cleared. "I hope you're right. I want everything to be perfect."

"Believe me, it is." Maria's doelike eyes scanned the premises. "Matt won't recognize his house, especially the living room."

"That's the object, my friend," Brittany said with a wide grin. "But I'm pooped and nervous."

Brittany couldn't get rid of the butterflies that fluttered in her stomach. They seemed to have taken up permanent residence.

She didn't know when the idea to redecorate Matt's modest house had first struck her. But it seemed to have fallen into place after he got a tip about some used equipment for sale cheap in Oklahoma. He was excited about that and the forthcoming insurance check.

The same afternoon he'd left, Brittany put her plan into action. Interior design had always been a hobby. She had decorated her daddy's house and enjoyed the challenge to the hilt. She'd also decorated several of her friends' homes.

So she decided she might as well make the best of his absence and redo his house, partly because it needed a facelift that only she could give it and partly because she wanted to do it for Matt. Why shouldn't he enjoy some of the amenities she was used to? She had the money to do it, which made it that much more fun.

The idea to include Maria had been spontaneous. While Maria had been stunned at the invitation to spend a day shopping, she'd accepted. Brittany knew she'd had a good time and that it had been good for her to leave Skipper with a sitter.

"When is Matt due back?" Maria asked, cutting into the companionable silence.

"Any minute now, actually."

Maria bounced up from the couch. "I should be going then."

Brittany laughed. "Why? Matt will be glad to see you."

"I know. But I need to pick up Skipper and get home before dark." She smiled. "Thanks again for a lovely time. I don't know when I've enjoyed myself more."

Brittany stood and placed her arms around Maria's thin shoulders. "Thank you for helping. I never could've gotten it done without you. I'll be in touch soon."

She had just walked into the kitchen and started the coffee when she heard Matt's truck. Her heart raced in anticipation. She couldn't wait to see his face and hear his praise.

She'd dressed for the occasion in a pair of gold leggings and top. The outfit drew attention to her curves as well as her red hair and fair skin. She hoped Matt would notice.

She positioned herself in the doorway between the living room and kitchen.

"Brittany?" he said as he walked into the room.

"Hi."

Matt stopped mid-stride and stared.

Her eyes followed the same course as his, saw what he was seeing. Soft yellow mini-blinds had taken the place of the flimsy dull drapes. White paneling had replaced the dark, thanks to a local painter. New pictures had displaced old ones.

The hodgepodge of furniture styles had been replaced with a luxurious green leather couch, love seat and chair. Lamps and other sundry items had either been replaced or added.

"I've also redone the bedrooms," Brittany said anxiously. "The only thing I haven't done is the kitchen, but—"

"Just who the hell do you think you are?"

"I...I just thought..." Brittany broke off abruptly, her explanation dammed behind a twist of pain.

"Who gave you the right to change my house?"

"I didn't think I needed permission." She pushed aside her rising panic and raised her voice to counter his. "After all, I live here, too."

"What's the matter?" he sneered. "It wasn't good enough for you the way it was?"

Brittany tipped her head and gazed at the ceiling, fighting the rawness in her throat. "No, that...that wasn't it at all."

"Then what was it?" he demanded, looming over her, his eyes blazing with fire.

"I...I just wanted..." Again her voice played out as she backed up, but not far. The knocking of her knees was so severe that it would have registered on the Richter scale.

"No! You didn't think. That's the problem. If you had, you wouldn't have changed my house." Matt's face looked like the devil incarnate's. "It was good enough for me, and by damn, it should have been good enough for you!"

"Go to hell!" she said, the words more violent for their softness. Then, without waiting for his response, she walked out of the room, her head held high. She wouldn't cry. She'd die before she'd give him the satisfaction of seeing how much he'd wounded her.

But when she got to their bedroom, the tears couldn't be denied. She lay across the bed. They poured down her face.

Brittany wished she could hate him. Maybe she did. For an instant her spirits brightened. She loved him, and that was what made his cruel rejection of her all the more painful.

Damn him and his pride, she cried silently, clutching the pillow against her breasts as if it was a lifeline.

"Brittany?"

"Go away." The sound was muffled.

"Look, I'm sorry." Matt paused and gulped a trembling breath. "I didn't mean to hurt your feelings. I acted like a jackass. So what else is new?"

His words spurred Brittany into a sitting position. Dragging her hands across her eyes, she walked to the door, jerked it open and stared at him.

"You've got that right." Her beautiful face was tight as metal. "You are a jackass."

Matt flashed her one of his rare smiles.

"But then I was wrong, too." Her voice shrank to almost nothing, and she avoided his gaze. "I should've talked it over with you so you—"

"Sh, it's all right."

"I never meant to imply that you're house wasn't good enough—"

"Hey, give it a rest. I like it. I like it a lot."

Brittany wasn't convinced. "Are you sure?"

"Come here," Matt muttered huskily, "and I'll show you how sure I am."

A heartbeat later, he folded her tightly against him and smiled. Only that smile never reached his eyes. Those eyes matched the bleakness of the starless sky.

"Brittany thinks Billy's behind our equipment problems."

Elmer's mouth fell open. "Billy?"

Matt smiled a humorless smile. "That's what I said. And now that I've thought about it, it makes sense."

Matt followed Elmer from the shed to the truck. They stood and continued to talk.

"Yeah, that'd work." Elmer rubbed his whiskers and glanced sideways at Matt. "We both know how he feels about you."

"So you're wondering why the hell I keep him around?"

"Something like that, only I think I figured that out. Guilt, right?"

"Right," Matt admitted ruefully.

"So what are you gonna do?"

"Watch the little s.o.b. like a shadow."

Elmer grinned; then the grin faded. "He don't look like he has enough smarts to do anything like that."

"I feel the same way."

"And didn't he come begging for money?"

"Yep, but that doesn't mean a thing. If he is behind it, he's probably not getting near what it's worth, hot or not."

"Especially if someone's working with him."

Matt's lips twisted. "If I find out he *is* involved, you can bet I'm going to see that the law puts him *under* the damn jail."

"By the way, how's the missus doing?"

Matt smiled inwardly. The moment Elmer had met Brittany, he'd been smitten. Matt hadn't been shocked. Brittany affected people like that. Hell, she'd affected him that way, too. The only problem was, he hadn't recovered.

"She's fine," Matt said more sharply than he intended.

Elmer opened his mouth to respond to Matt's retort when the crunch of automobile tires interrupted them.

Matt spun, thinking it was Brittany. She was due back from Longview, where she'd been working on a case.

When he saw the Lincoln Continental, he breathed an expletive.

"I take it your visitor's someone you don't want to see."

"If my gut instinct is right, which it usually is, that's my father-in-law."

Elmer followed Matt's gaze, then whistled through his half-rotten teeth. "One of those, huh?"

The way he said "those," as though it were a contagious disease, brought a brief but genuine smile to Matt's lips.

"I wouldn't know, not really. I've never met the man."

Again Elmer's jaw flapped open.

"My wife's never seen fit to introduce us."

Elmer looked at his boss a long moment, then climbed in his truck. "I'm shoving off. You got other fish to fry."

"Yeah," Matt muttered sardonically.

Just as Elmer backed up and headed down the drive, the man got out of his car. He was well dressed and manicured. Matt suspected he never walked out the door any other way.

"Great," Matt said under his breath. Things were fragile enough between him and Brittany. They certainly didn't need another complication.

But what could he do? After all, the man *was* his father-in-law.

Brittany's breath hitched in her lungs when she saw her daddy's car in the drive. Granted, she had planned for Matt and her daddy to meet soon. But she'd wanted it at her convenience. She'd wanted to be prepared to handle any problems that might arise with such a meeting.

Today she wasn't prepared. The day had been a long and tiring one. The case she'd been working on was difficult, and so were the parties involved. She didn't need any more hassles.

She and Matt were still walking on eggshells around each other even though it had been three weeks since their blowup over the house. However, they had made great strides in patching things up between them— mostly in bed.

How long had Walter been there? she wondered, killing the engine and getting out of the car. She had a hand on the front doorknob when she looked up and saw them walking out of the workshop.

As they approached her, Brittany tried not to wince visibly.

"Surprised, I bet," Walter said, and leaned over and kissed her on the cheek.

Brittany's gaze strayed to Matt. He winked. Instantly, she relaxed and smiled.

"When did you get here, Daddy?"

Walter faced Matt. "How long have I been here?"

"Oh, 'bout an hour, I'd say."

"Matt was kind enough to show me around the place. In fact, we've had quite a nice visit."

Brittany clamped her teeth together so that her mouth wouldn't flop open. But Matt knew what she was thinking.

His lips twitched. "You can relax. We didn't go behind the shed and strap on our guns. Instead, Walter asked to see my operation, and I showed him."

"That's right," Walter chimed in. "I decided it was past time I met my son-in-law, and since I had business in these parts, I decided to stop by."

Brittany shook her head to clear it. "Well, I'm glad you did, only—"

"Stop spluttering, child, and invite me in. I'm dying of thirst."

Ten minutes later they were in the living room, sipping coffee.

Walter emptied his cup, set it on the coffee table and looked directly at Matt. "If you've got another minute, I have something I'd like to talk over with you."

His tone was casual, Brittany thought, too casual.

Matt, who stood by the fireplace, straightened slightly, but said nothing.

"What is it?" Brittany asked.

Walter kept his eyes fixed on Matt. "How would you like to move to Tyler, go to work for my company? I have to say I'm impressed, and since you're my daughter's husband, what could be better?"

Breath escaped from Matt's lungs like air from a punctured tire. But he still didn't say a word. He merely looked at Brittany.

The room filled with a suffocating tension.

Walter stood and looked at Brittany. "The doctor's told me I need to take it easy or else."

"Oh, Daddy," Brittany wailed. "Why haven't—"

Walter held up his hand and stopped her flow of words. "I'm not going to the cemetery, despite what my gloom-and-doom doctors say. But I do plan to slow down. Why don't the two of you talk over my offer. I need to go, anyway."

"But Daddy..." Brittany spluttered.

He leaned over and once again pecked her on the cheek. "I'll see myself out."

When they were alone, Matt turned to her and asked, "Was this your idea? Did you put him up to asking me?"

Brittany let the angry questions hang in the air, then said, "Would it be so terrible if I did? I think it's a wonderful idea."

Matt's face swelled with rage. "Well, I think it stinks."

Brittany felt a new heaviness inside her. "Won't you even think about it?"

"No," he said, baring his teeth. "You can be at your daddy's beck and call if you want to, but not me."

A long and heavy sigh came from her. "I guess this means we're about to have another argument."

"No, that's not what it means at all, because there's nothing to argue about. I'm sorry his health is poor. But I'm *not* going to work for your daddy." Matt's nostrils flared. "Not now. Not ever!"

He turned and stormed out the door.

Sixteen

What next? Brittany asked herself.

First there had been the confrontation about the house, then her daddy and the job.

Matt barely talked to her. He shut her out completely, and there was no way to reach him.

He continued to blame her, thinking she'd gone behind his back to Walter. She denied it. Her daddy's offer was just as much a shock to her as it was to him.

Matt didn't believe her. She wasn't sure she believed it herself. Walter didn't make rash decisions. He weighed every detail beforehand. Only this time he'd fooled her.

Maybe he'd told the truth when he said health problems were forcing him to slow down. She doubted that. No, he had another motive.

But for whatever reason her daddy made the offer, Matt should have taken it as a compliment. He didn't. If she had learned one thing about her husband, he was in every sense his own man. And a proud one, to boot. So proud that he took Walter's offer as an insult.

Because she feared this latest incident would cost her her marriage, Brittany was determined to make him listen to reason.

The next morning she set the alarm and got up so she could talk to him before he left for the woods. She walked into the living room and found Matt sitting on the side of the couch where he'd slept the night before...

His head was bent, and his face was in his hands. Her heart turned over and she ached to go to him, to beg him if necessary to forgive her. She stepped toward him, and he looked up.

"What do you want?" he asked, his voice remote, his face like stone.

She winced at the stab of pain that took her breath. "I...think we should talk."

"I told you, we have nothing to talk about." His eyebrows were drawn together, his face pinched.

The bottom of her stomach fell away. "I didn't know Daddy was going to make you an offer."

"Maybe not. But you were damn well for it, weren't you?"

Brittany tried to swallow, but her mouth was too dry. "I worry about you—"

"Bull," he spat, lunging to his feet. "You worry about yourself, about being away from Daddy and all your other highfalutin friends—"

"No! That's not true."

Sweat broke out over his forehead, but the controlled expression on his face did not change. "Then I guess you'll just have to prove that, won't you..."

But he didn't give her the chance to prove it. He stayed gone from daylight till dark. He was so tired when he came in that he barely managed to eat a few bites before taking a shower and falling into bed.

And the fact that she was on vacation made matters worse. She had nothing but time on her hands. She was lonesome. That was why she decided to cook a full meal. She studied a cookbook, planned a meal, then went to the grocery store.

Matt told her that morning he would be in early. As she waited for him, she scrutinized her handiwork again. The table was decorated with their wedding pottery and glasses. A bouquet of fresh flowers, as a centerpiece, added the final and perfect touch.

Not bad, Brittany told herself. She'd decided against adding candles. She wouldn't want him to get the idea she was trying to seduce him into forgiving her.

But that was exactly what she was doing. She was dressed for the part, as well. She had on a peach silk lounging suit that showed off her figure to perfection. She'd worn it once before, and she'd begged Matt *not* to tear it in his haste to get it off her.

Her pulse raced when she thought of what had happened next.

"What's going on here?"

Brittany swung around and slapped a hand against her heart. "I . . . I didn't hear you."

Matt's gaze shifted to the table. "I would ask if we're having company, but since there are only two plates . . ." His voice trailed off.

"I fixed dinner . . . for us."

His eyes seemed to delve inside her. Brittany's heart kicked into double time.

"I'll shower then," he muttered.

"I'd like to go to the woods with you in the morning."

They had finished eating and had cleared the table. Brittany was drinking coffee and Matt was sipping a beer.

Matt stared at her for a long moment. "Why?"

"Because I enjoyed myself the last time."

"Liar," he said softly.

Brittany flushed. "I am not lying." She felt her temper rise, the last thing she wanted. She took a deep breath. "Also, I'd like to give a party, get to know your friends and neighbors."

"Good try."

She frowned. "I don't understand."

"Yeah, you do."

"Since when did you become clairvoyant?" she snapped.

Matt lifted his brows, but when he spoke his tone was as soft as hers had been harsh. "Your face gives you away."

"Oh, really?" she said, looking upward as if to pray for divine guidance. He was the most stubborn...

"All right," he said.

Brittany lowered her head abruptly. "You mean it?" She had no idea what made him change his mind, but it didn't matter. As the old cliché went, she wasn't about to look a gift horse in the mouth.

"Be ready in the morning." His smile lasted only a second, but she was struck by it. "We'll talk about the party later."

Later. What a wonderful ring that word had to it.

He drained the last of his beer, then got up. "Thanks for the meal. It was good."

"You sound surprised."

"Well..."

She laughed self-consciously.

Her eyes searched his face and glimpsed a flash of longing in his eyes. Then, before she could say anything else, he turned and walked toward the door.

"Matt?"

Her soft voice stopped him in his tracks. He pivoted and waited for her to continue, his eyes hooded.

"Nothing," she whispered into the tense silence.

His face looked stretched, almost gaunt. "I'll see you in the morning," he said roughly.

Brittany hadn't slept. Now it was time to get up. Last night it had been on the tip of her tongue to beg Matt to share her bed, but that look in his eyes had stopped her cold.

He still hadn't forgiven her, yet she sensed he was coming around, that he was thawing somewhat. The fact that he'd waited until later to go to the woods was evidence of that. She was pleased at his thoughtfulness.

Too, Brittany remembered and clung to that look of longing she'd seen in his eyes. It was her lifeline.

She scrambled out of bed, dressed in jeans, long-sleeved shirt, so as not to blister, and tennis shoes. She put on minimal makeup and ran a comb through her curls.

When she made her way into the kitchen, Matt was waiting for her. She stopped for a moment and breathed in the scent of his cologne.

"Hi," he said.

There was the slightest tremor in his voice. It gave her comfort. She smiled. "Good morning."

"Your coffee's on the table."

"Thanks," she said, reaching for it. "I take it you're ready to go." She watched him over the rim of her cup.

"It's time, don't you think? It's nearly eight o'clock."

They reached the side door, and the phone rang.

Brittany groaned, but it never occurred to her not to answer it. Rushing into the room, she lifted the receiver.

She listened, then said in a strident voice, "Today?" She listened again, then frowned. "I'm sorry. I forgot."

Matt used the counter for a prop and watched her, his expression wary.

Shortly, Brittany placed the receiver on the hook and muttered, "Damn."

"Walter?" Matt's tone was brisk.

"Yes," she said, her face troubled.

"Is something wrong?"

"No. There's nothing wrong. It's just..."

"Spit it out, Brittany. I'm a big boy— I can take it."

Ignoring the edge in his voice, she said, "Daddy's having a political fund-raising dinner tonight—"

Matt pushed away from the cabinet. "So? What's that got to do with you?"

Brittany took a steadying breath. "I promised him a long time ago that I'd act as hostess."

"I take it you're going home, then."

"Yes."

"Are you coming back?"

Silence, sudden and total, descended over the room.

The fact that he even asked her cut to the core. But she wouldn't let it deter her from her mission. Since they had stayed together after she lost the baby, she had felt they had a chance to make their marriage work, to have a real marriage. And somewhere along the way, she had convinced herself that he had to love her or he wouldn't have stayed.

But the time had come to hear him say the words, to tell her that he loved her. Now.

"Can you give me a good reason I should?" Brittany's voice trembled. There. She'd said it; she'd opened the door, made it easy. It was up to him. Say it, Matt! Say you love me and that you don't want to live without me.

The seconds turned into a minute.

Something was wrong. Terribly wrong. He stared at her as if he'd never seen her before. She felt cold suddenly. And brittle. If she moved or touched anything she feared she would break into a million pieces.

"Matt," she said in a strangled tone. "Answer me."

His hands dropped to his side. "No, there's no reason for you to come back."

Brittany's eyes, filled with horror, steadied on his face. She shook her head from side to side, denying what she was hearing.

"No, you...don't, can't mean that."

"Trust me. I mean it." The words were barely spoken, as if they had been dug out of him.

Her soundless cry met with a stark silence.

"How can you..." Brittany couldn't go on. This couldn't be happening. Pure agony twisted inside her like a knife.

Matt looked away, his stance unyielding. "Go back where you belong, Brittany." He faced her again. "For both our sakes. You belong with your daddy— in his world, not mine."

Tears burned Brittany's eyes while an awesome force seemed to press her from all sides, sucking the very lifeblood out of her. "Matt...for god's sake—"

"Go, dammit! Just go."

As if he'd struck her, she recoiled.

He turned and walked out the door, closing it softly behind him.

Brittany reached blindly for the wall. Her shoulders shook; she gulped wrenching sobs. She kept flinching inside her skin. Oh, God, was this the end? Was her marriage over? Just like that? *No!* Everything in her screamed. *No!*

But she knew better. Matt not only didn't love her, he didn't even want her. With the truth came the emptiness. It was over.

He was over.

Seventeen

—

"Son of a bitch!"

Matt's mumbled curse echoed off the walls of the workshop. But he scarcely noticed he'd spoken out loud. He was too busy assessing the damage done to his place.

Someone had walked in and helped themselves to tools and other equipment critical to his work. The guilty party hadn't stopped there; the building had been trashed. It looked as though a small tornado had ripped through the place.

Billy Frost. Matt felt sure the culprit was Billy Frost, but he couldn't prove it. The last time Billy approached him was three days ago. Billy had asked for money. Again. But why? If he was indeed behind the thefts, then why would he need money? Maybe Elmer was right—maybe he was getting rooked on the deal, or maybe he enjoyed being a thorn in Matt's side, determined not to let him forget the accident that killed Tim.

Of course, Matt had turned Billy down flat. No more money, he'd said. Billy had gotten furious.

"You owe me!" he'd shouted, his face red. "You owe me for what you did to my brother."

"I don't owe *you* a damn thing," Matt responded, "except a good tanning if you don't get out of my sight."

Billy, apparently having heard the edge to Matt's voice, didn't say anything.

"And what's more," Matt added, "if you don't watch your mouth, you're going to talk yourself right out of a job."

"You don't scare me," Billy sneered, all the while backing up, making his tough talk just that and nothing more.

Matt strode toward him, his lips stretched into a thin, tight line. "Listen up, once and for all," he said. "The only reason I keep you around is because of Tim. But there's a limit to my patience, and I've nearly reached it. So be warned."

Billy had looked as if he wanted to say something, but wisely hadn't. Mumbling to himself, he'd sulked off.

Now, as Matt took a thorough mental inventory, he reminded himself that Brittany had seen Billy's true colors from the beginning. He paused in his thoughts and recoiled as if he'd been kicked in the solar plexus. He mustn't allow himself to dwell on *her* right now. Ha, that was a joke without the humor.

Actually, he'd dwelled on little else since Brittany had left four weeks ago today.

Sam nuzzled his nose, then sat and stared at Matt.

Matt rubbed his head.

Sam thumped his tail.

Matt's smile was more a grimace. "Come on, let's go call the sheriff."

The evenings were the killers. Tonight was no different. The sheriff had left only a short while before, promising to question Billy, especially as he'd been caught around Matt's place one other time.

Matt showered, dressed, then walked out of the bedroom and into the kitchen. But he no longer felt hungry.

He felt an emptiness that no amount of food could affect. Regardless of where he went in the house, he saw Brittany. It was that way in the woods, too. She flashed before his eyes at the most inopportune moments, causing him to make mistakes.

Matt took a deep breath. His heart hurt. He could still smell her perfume; he thought it must be embedded in his flesh. He could feel her lips on his, soft and burning.

The palms of his hands were suddenly slick with sweat, and the pain in his soul was almost unbearable.

He had to get hold of himself. After all, he was the one who had sent her away. He should have been prepared for the shock. Only he wasn't. He was wound so tight, the best part of him was in danger of breaking apart.

Matt stalked into the kitchen and grabbed a beer out of the refrigerator. He knew drinking wasn't the answer, and until this evening, he hadn't used it as a crutch.

Tonight threatened to be the pits, maybe the worst night he'd had. And dear lord, he'd had some bad ones. He couldn't begin to count the times he'd waked himself up rubbing the sheet beside him, thinking she was still there.

He took another healthy swig of the beer. The need for Brittany boiled his blood. He wanted to touch her, be inside her, hear her moan, hear her cry out. But more than anything, he wanted to hear her laughter, watch her sashay around the place as if she owned it, feel the sting of her sharp tongue.

If only he'd handled things differently. If only he hadn't expected too much too soon from her. From himself. After the baby had died, something seemed to have shattered inside him, and nothing was ever the same.

Matt felt sure she was sorry she'd married him. So he thought he was doing her a favor by sending her away. Brittany had never belonged in his world. He'd known that the minute she'd walked into his house. She was like an expensive and exotic hothouse plant that had been uprooted and replanted in the wild.

She had begun to wither before his eyes. He couldn't let that happen.

But maybe he had been too hasty. Maybe she was made of stronger stuff than he'd given her credit for.

Had *he* been the weak one? The coward, afraid to share himself, his emotions with someone else? No, dammit! He wasn't a coward. He wanted a home and family. But only if he could have Brittany.

So prove it, a voice taunted. Get up and go tell her you love her and that you're not worth a damn without her. Even if you have to beg, tell her.

Fear squeezed his heart until he couldn't get his breath. Regardless of the outcome, he couldn't live with himself if he didn't try.

His mind buzzed. He had to cut another load for the mill at dawn. The minute he got through, he'd head for Tyler. And Brittany.

Suddenly, he no longer felt a zillion years old.

Brittany bent over the toilet and lost everything in her stomach. When she was done, she stood. Though she was weak, she felt much better.

A virus. Or a broken heart. She wasn't sure which was the cause. She knew she wasn't pregnant because she had started her period yesterday. So she opted for the broken heart. Grief could turn your inside out.

Miscarrying had proved that. Now she was experiencing it again with Matt. Tears welled in her eyes. She brushed them away. If she started crying, she wouldn't be able to stop.

Brittany brushed her teeth and repaired her makeup, then walked into the office. Wade was perched on the edge of her desk thumbing through some papers he had in his hand.

He looked up. "My god, you look awful."

"I don't feel good," Brittany responded coldly.

"Ah, hell, Brittany, loosen up. We all can't keep taking it on the chin because you and Matt—"

Brittany glared at him. "That's a cheap shot, and you know it."

"You're right," Wade said uneasily, shifting his gaze. "And believe it or not, I didn't come in here to pick a fight."

"Then why did you come?" Exhausted, Brittany sat behind her desk.

"I came to pass you a compliment, actually."

"Are you serious?"

"Yes, I am, though I'll have to admit, you've surprised the hell out of me."

"One thing about you, Wade, you have a way with words."

Wade lit a cigarette. He drew in a lung full of smoke and let it trail out slowly.

Brittany frowned, then batted the air. "Please, put that foul thing out. You know how I feel about you smoking in here." More so now since she was sick to her stomach.

Wade flushed and ground out the cigarette in an ashtray on the coffee table.

"So tell me how I've surprised you?" Brittany didn't particularly care, not really. Her head felt as if it were going to split. Still, it wasn't like Wade to think anything good about her, much less say it.

"Your work. It's been damn good. You've settled some cases that I never thought would ever be settled—and in our favor, too."

Only because I'd have lost my mind if I hadn't had my work. She kept her thoughts to herself. She didn't dare expose her pain for the world to see.

"Thanks, Wade," she finally said, rubbing her forehead.

His eyes narrowed. "You sure you're all right?"

"I'm fine." She smiled shakily and rose to her feet. "No, I'm not fine. I have a pounding headache. If you don't mind, I'm going home; I'll take my work with me."

Wade bounced off the desk. "Forget the work. Just go home and fix yourself a toddie for the body and crawl into bed."

"I just might do that," Brittany said, and reached for her briefcase.

Home.

It was her solace, where she could lick her wounds in private and none would be the wiser. But others were the wiser. She hadn't fooled anyone, not really, especially not her friends, not her co-workers and not her daddy.

Broken hearts were hard to disguise, even though she did her best. But she admitted that at times she was hard to get along with. There was some truth in what Wade said.

Brittany was home two days before she mustered the courage to tell her daddy about the breakup of her marriage. The dreaded words, "I told you so," kept her mum.

He didn't say them, but he *did* demand to know what happened. While she tried to decide how to tell him, he asked, "Did my job offer have anything to do with your leaving?"

"Yes and no," Brittany said with a quaver in her voice.

"What kind of answer is that?"

Finding it impossible to divulge the painful details, she answered his question with a question. "Why did you make that offer, Daddy?"

"I did it for you," Walter said stiffly.

"No, you didn't," she countered, peering at him with pain-filled eyes. "You did for you." Voicing that ugly thought turned her stomach. "You still can't bear the thought of your daughter being married to a redneck logger. You're worried about what your associates, your friends at the country club are saying, aren't you?"

Walter straightened. "What if I am?"

"And what about the doctor's order to slow down? Is that a lot of hot air, too?"

"Not...exactly," Walter hedged. "Regardless of what the doctor said, I do plan to curtail my work load."

"But you had no intention of letting Matt have a responsible job." It was a statement, not a question.

She saw Walter's face tighten as she hit a nerve. He didn't say anything. He didn't have to. His silence had spoken louder than words ever could have. And had cracked her heart a little wider....

Now, as Brittany pulled her car into her garage, she noticed it was raining. A short time later, she sat in her robe with her feet folded under her and watched through the French doors as the rain pounded the deck outside.

She wondered if it was raining at Matt's place. In a wretched whisper, she sobbed his name.

The finality, the ruthlessness, the unfairness of it, had smashed her heart to such a degree that she wasn't sure she would recover.

She'd been devastated when she'd miscarried, but the pain now was worse. The baby had never been part of her life; she'd never held it in her arms, had never kissed it. But she had Matt.

He was flesh and blood, and she missed him with every fiber of her being. Nothing made sense without him. So why had she let him push her out of his life?

Brittany sat up suddenly, as though she'd been slapped. Why, indeed? She had fought from day one to keep their marriage together. She had vowed not to give up, to keep fighting until he admitted that he loved her.

Well, she certainly hadn't lived up to that vow. What she should've done was call his bluff, make him look her square in the eye and tell her he didn't love her. Instead, she had folded like a flimsy tent in a hurricane wind.

Brittany stood quickly, too quickly. Her head swam, and for a minute she thought she might faint. Damn, she needed to eat something, even if it was only crackers and a cold drink.

There wasn't time. She'd made up her mind what she was going to do and she didn't have a second to lose...or she just might lose her nerve.

She dashed into her bedroom, tossed the robe on the bed and slipped into a pair of jeans, shirt and Reeboks. With keys in hand, she dashed to the front door, only to hear the bell chime in her ear. She jerked open the door.

"Daddy!" Her shocked tone conveyed her surprise.

"Were you going somewhere?"

"Yes, as a matter of fact, I was." Brittany held her ground.

He sighed. "I suggest you come in and hear what I have to say first."

An alarm went off in her brain. It wasn't so much what he said as the way he said it. "All . . . right."

They walked into the living room, but neither took a seat. Brittany looked at her daddy hard, hoping his features would shed some light on what he was thinking. They didn't. They remained remote and in place.

She smothered a sigh, then said, "What is it you have to say?"

He rubbed his forehead. "It's about Matt."

Brittany reached for the chair behind her for support. Her legs trembled. "What . . . what about Matt?"

"He's been hurt."

"Oh, no!"

"A loader overturned and pinned him underneath."

She fell into the chair, clutched at her stomach and waited for it to stop lurching.

"But he's going to live—the doctors are certain of it."

"Thank God," she wheezed. "But how did you know? I mean—"

"A man named Elmer Cayhill called the office, and when they refused to give him your home phone number, he told the secretary about Matt." Walter paused. "I thought I should be the one to tell you."

Brittany stood. "I have to go to him," she whispered, feeling as if the weight on her chest might crush her before she could get to the door.

Walter stepped in front of her. "I don't think that's a good idea."

"What!"

He pursed his lips. "I think you should leave well enough alone."

"What...what are you saying?" Tears flooded her eyes so that she could barely see his face. "He's my husband."

"Soon to be ex."

Brittany flinched. But she recovered and said, "That doesn't matter. For now, he's still my husband."

"For god's sake, Brittany. Let it go. Let him go. Now that he's out of your life, let him stay. He's not good enough for you. He never has been and never will be."

"How would you know what's good for me?" she cried.

He seemed taken aback at the venom in her voice. "I'm your father, that's how."

"Oh, please, spare me."

His face turned red, then purple. "Don't you dare talk to me like that. I know what's best for you, and I forbid you to—"

"You forbid me? That's a joke. You can't forbid me to do anything, Daddy. Not anymore, that is." Tears ran down her face. "I love you, and lord knows I've tried to please you all of my life because I thought that by being perfect you would love me back.''

"Brittany...don't."

"No!" she flared. "Let me finish. But I finally realized that nothing I did was going to ever be good enough." She sniffed back the tears. "I don't mind, though, not anymore, because I have Matt. I still want your love, but it's no longer the most important thing to me.

"But Matt's is. And if he'll have me, I intend to spend the rest of my life loving him."

Later, while her car dispensed of the highway miles, she realized there had been tears on her daddy's face. Or had she imagined them?

Eighteen

The hospital smell was an assault on Brittany's senses. She'd been in the waiting room for thirty minutes, and still she couldn't escape the offensive smell.

While she longed to go outside, breathe fresh air, dynamite couldn't have budged her, not until she talked to Matt's doctor, then saw Matt himself.

What was taking the doctor so long? she asked herself, trying to curb her fear along with her irritation. When she had arrived, she had expected to see Elmer and possibly Maria. The nurse had told her that Elmer had just left, after he'd learned that Matt was out of danger. She knew if she called Maria she'd come immediately. First, though, she wanted to talk to the doctor, to reassure herself that Matt was indeed out of danger.

Weakly, Brittany leaned her head against the facing of the window and toyed with her lower lip. If something happened to Matt, she wouldn't want to live.

"Mrs. Diamond?"

Brittany swung around and stared into the face of a tall, thin man in a white coat. The coat matched his hair, she thought inanely. "Yes?" Her heart was in her throat.

"I'm Dr. Kent."

"How...how is Matt?"

"He came through the surgery just fine, although we had to remove his spleen."

"Oh, no," she whispered, horrified.

"There were a few other internal injuries, but none life threatening."

"So are you saying he'll recover one hundred percent?"

"Yes, except for—"

"What?" Brittany interrupted, feeling her heart sink to her toes.

Dr. Kent's features were sober. "There's a possibility he could be paralyzed from the waist down."

Brittany didn't so much as flinch. "For how long?"

"Maybe as long as he lives."

"No." It was a pained, shocked, gut-wrenching gasp. She almost crumpled at the man's feet.

"Mrs. Diamond, are you all right?" His kind features twisted with concern.

Brittany eased down on the couch that was behind her and looked at him while fighting the tears. "When will you know?"

"I can't say. For the next two days he'll be sleeping mostly, drifting in and out. We'll know more when the anesthetic wears off."

"Can I see him?"

"Of course."

Brittany stood and held out her hand. "Thank you, Doctor."

He patted her hand. "Think positive, my dear."

She entered Matt's room and tiptoed to the side of the bed. Except for a scratch on one side of his face and a bruise on the other, Matt looked like his old self.

She leaned over and gently kissed his forehead. He stirred but didn't open his eyes. Tears burned hers as she sat in the chair beside the bed and forced herself to face reality.

Matt could be paralyzed. Forever. She placed a hand to her mouth to keep from crying. Oh, God, no. Not to walk again, not to be able to make love—*he* wouldn't be able to stand it.

Brittany lifted her head suddenly, as though to keep from drowning. And what of her? Could she stand it? Could she stand by him, not just now, but always? Did she have what it took? If not, now was the time to leave. She could get up and walk out, return to Tyler, to her daddy, to her old way of life, and Matt would be none the wiser.

Or she could stand by the man she had married for better or worse, in sickness and in health, not for what she wanted him to be, but for what he was.

The decision was clear. But then it always had been. He might be paralyzed, but she loved Matt, and that love, if he'd have her back, just might work miracles that no doctor or modern medicine could.

"I love you, my darling," she whispered. "And I won't let you down."

For the next two days, Brittany remained by his side, though she was certain he never knew it. When he started to moan and his eyes glazed with pain, the nurses gave him a shot.

But the long hours with only short doses of sleep were wearing on Brittany. That was when Maria insisted she go home and sleep. Elmer agreed.

"We'll sit with him," Maria said gently. "We won't leave him. Now, will that put your mind to rest?"

Brittany nodded, then grabbed Maria's hand. "If there's any change, you'll call me?"

"Of course," Maria said in a soothing voice as if she were talking to a child. "Now go on, get out of here."

Brittany had slept much longer than she intended. She had to admit, though, she felt much better, more able to cope with what lay ahead.

After Maria and Elmer had practically pushed her out of Matt's room, she had gone to the nearest motel and straight to bed.

Now, as she stood in front of his door, she felt her knees knock together.

It had been three days since his surgery, and she expected Matt to be awake and fully in charge of his faculties. She had no idea how he would react to her presence.

Brittany tapped on the door.

"It's open." His tone was quarrelsome, at best.

She stiffened her shoulders, then pushed open the heavy door.

Matt sat in the bed with his pajama top open to the waist. If the circumstances had been different, she might have smiled. He hated pajamas, choosing to sleep in his briefs.

Circumstances weren't different and she didn't smile, especially when she saw the scowl on his face.

"What are you doing here?" he asked, the scowl deepening. He took advantage of her silence and added, "If you've come just because I got hurt, then—"

"I came because I love you."

He opened his mouth, then clamped it shut while disbelief registered in his eyes. "I don't want your pity."

She'd been afraid he would reject her; she had warned herself that her mission might backfire. But now that it had—oh, God, it hurt. It hurt so bad, she wanted to die.

With a muttered cry, Brittany turned and stumbled toward the door.

"Please...I didn't mean...please don't go." Matt's voice sounded broken.

She stopped, and ever so slowly turned around. They stared at each other.

"I love you, Matt," she whispered again. "And even if you are paralyzed—"

"Paralyzed? Is that what you said?"

Brittany couldn't speak; she could only nod.

"Have you seen the doctor this morning?" Matt asked.

"No...no I haven't," she said around the huge lump in her throat.

"I'm not paralyzed, Brittany."

It took several seconds for his softly spoken words to penetrate her somewhat befuddled brain. But when they did, she laughed and cried at the same time, murmuring, "Thank God. Oh, thank God."

Only Matt wasn't laughing. He was staring at her with a strange expression on his face. "Are you saying you thought I was paralyzed?"

"Dr. Kent...said there was a chance you could be."

"And knowing that, you were willing to stay?"

Her gaze never wavered. "I never could have *not* stayed."

"Brittany—I love you, and I was coming to tell you that, to beg you to forgive me, to beg for another chance—"

"Oh, Matt," she cried, rushing toward him.

"No!"

She stopped, dumbfounded.

He grinned. "Stay there. I'm coming to you."

Even if she wanted, Brittany couldn't have moved. She smiled through her tears and held out her arms. Seconds later, he dove into them.

The nurse found them still locked in each other's arms.

"Is that a new robe?"

Brittany flashed her husband a demure look. "Mm,

you noticed." She purposely ran her hand over the turquoise silk as if stroking it.

His eyes darkened. "Oh, I noticed all right. I notice everything about you."

They were in the bedroom at Matt's house, although it was no longer just Matt's house, but *their* house. Three months had passed since Matt's accident, and finally Matt had returned to work.

His recovery had been slow, but without complications. Through it all, Brittany had stayed by his side. They took long walks, they swam in the creek, they read books together. But most of all they loved and they laughed.

The only real excitement was Billy Frost's arrest. He had been caught in the act of stealing equipment. Once he was arrested, he admitted to stealing Matt's, as well.

Brittany had never been happier, and neither had Matt. That was why she scrutinized him so closely now. He had come in exhausted, and after eating dinner, Brittany had insisted he go to bed early. She hadn't liked the tired lines around his eyes and mouth. However, the doctor had assured her that he was fit to do anything he wanted to. But since Matt couldn't be trusted to keep his actions in the perimeter of reasonable, she worried.

"Are you sure you didn't overdo it today?"

Matt kicked his jeans aside. "Nag, nag, nag."

Brittany made a face, then picked up her hairbrush and pulled it absently through her short curls. Her mind wasn't on her hair. It was on Matt, who crossed to the side of the bed, clad only in his briefs, and sat down.

Brittany felt his eyes on her as she continued to brush her hair.

"I love you," he said, his eyes filled with passion.

She paused and caught her breath.

"I don't think I'll ever get tired of saying that."

"I love you, too," she said. "And I know I won't get tired of hearing it."

"By the way, did I tell you that you look great in that robe?"

"No." She placed the brush on the dresser.

He stood, never taking his eyes off her. "But you look better without it, you know."

His voice and leering look brought a smile to Brittany's lips. "You're bad, Matthew Diamond."

"And you love it."

She untied the robe and stood before him, completely naked. The lamplight danced across her skin. She heard Matt's sharp intake of breath as his eyes roamed greedily over her.

"Do you notice anything different about me?"

"Only that you're the loveliest creature I've ever seen," he said in a strangled voice.

"Is that all?"

"Suppose you come over here and tell me what I'm supposed to see."

"All right," she said.

But when she reached him, he pulled her down beside him on the bed. Words were forgotten as his mouth closed over hers.

He released her lips slowly, only to move to a breast. The wanting was sharp inside her, the pleasure edged by a need that knew no boundaries.

"I'm crazy when I'm not with you." He stroked her back and lingered at her hip. "You make me feel alive again."

"Show me," Brittany urged.

Matt sensed her mood and matched it. He shifted her onto her back, then rose above her and entered her, easily, gently.

Although she hadn't expected anything more than a special closeness, she climaxed within a minute. Not deeply, just a rush of flawless pleasure. However, when it happened a second time, moments before he spilled inside her, she cried out with delight, a delight that blended with his.

"Are you awake?"

Matt's raspy voice interrupted Brittany's slow descent into sleep. She snuggled against his chest, and his hold tightened.

"By the way, your daddy called today."

"Oh. What did he want?"

"You, of course."

Her fingertips massaged the nape of his neck. "I wish we could all—"

"I invited him to dinner tomorrow night."

Brittany's hand stilled. "You did?"

"Yep, and he accepted, too." Matt tweaked her on the nose. "I kinda felt sorry for him. He sounded—oh, I don't know—sort of blue."

"He is blue. He knows he screwed up trying to keep me away from you, and he's trying to make up."

"And you're giving him a hard time?"

"So are you."

"Yeah, but he's not my daddy."

"He's your daddy-in-law."

He nuzzled her neck. "Okay, I surrender. We'll both do better, try harder to include him."

"He never calls now that he doesn't tell me he loves me."

"'Bout time he realized how special you are."

"Matt, are you sure you haven't noticed something different about me?" Her voice sank lower.

He pulled back slightly. "Is something wrong?"

She smiled. "No, nothing's wrong. I'm pregnant."

Silence stretched through the room.

"You're glad, aren't you?" Brittany asked anxiously, and looked into the depth of his eyes. Something there stole her breath.

"Oh, Brittany, love, of course I'm glad." Matt leaned over and placed his lips against her stomach. "How could you think otherwise?"

Flutters of pleasure darted through her.

Matt lifted his head. "How far along are you?"

"Three and a half months. I was pregnant before the accident, only I didn't know it. I thought my period had started and just assumed everything was normal. But it wasn't. I only spotted and that was all."

"Does your daddy know?"

"No. I thought we'd tell him together. Later."

"Why later?"

"Because...I'm scared..." Her voice cracked. "I'm so afraid after—"

"Sh," he said. "Don't say it. Don't think it. Everything is going to be all right, you'll see."

She placed her palms against his cheeks and searched his eyes. "I love you."

"Don't ever leave me again," he pleaded. "Stay with me as long as I live."

"As long as we both shall live," Brittany promised.

* * * * *

This is the season of giving, and Silhouette proudly offers you its sixth annual Christmas collection.

SILHOUETTE

Christmas Stories

1991

Experience the joys of a holiday romance and treasure these heartwarming stories by four award-winning Silhouette authors:

Phyllis Halldorson—"A Memorable Noel"
Peggy Webb—"I Heard the Rabbits Singing"
Naomi Horton—"Dreaming of Angels"
Heather Graham Pozzessere—"The Christmas Bride"

Discover this yuletide celebration—sit back and enjoy Silhouette's Christmas gift of love.

YOU'VE ASKED FOR IT, YOU'VE GOT IT! MAN OF THE MONTH: 1992

ONLY FROM

SILHOUETTE® Desire™

You just couldn't get enough of them, those sexy men from Silhouette Desire—twelve sinfully sexy, delightfully devilish heroes. Some will make you sweat, some will make you sigh... but every long, lean one of them will have you swooning. So here they are, men we couldn't resist bringing to you for one more year....

A KNIGHT IN TARNISHED ARMOR
by Ann Major in January

THE BLACK SHEEP
by Laura Leone in February

THE CASE OF THE MESMERIZING BOSS
by Diana Palmer in March

DREAM MENDER
by Sheryl Woods in April

WHERE THERE IS LOVE
by Annette Broadrick in May

BEST MAN FOR THE JOB
by Dixie Browning in June

Don't let these men get away! *Man of the Month*, only in Silhouette Desire.

MOM92JJ-1

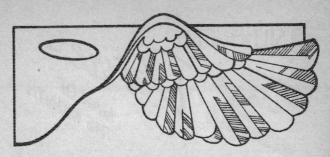

Angels Everywhere!

Everything's turning up angels at Silhouette. In November, Ann Williams's ANGEL ON MY SHOULDER (IM #408, $3.29) features a heroine who's absolutely heavenly—and we mean that literally! Her name is Cassandra, and once she comes down to earth, her whole picture of life—and love—undergoes a pretty radical change.

Then, in December, it's time for ANGEL FOR HIRE (D #680, $2.79) from Justine Davis. This time it's hero Michael Justice who brings a touch of out-of-this-world magic to the story. Talk about a match made in heaven . . . !

Look for both these spectacular stories wherever you buy books. But look soon—because they're going to be flying off the shelves as if they had wings!

If you can't find these books where you shop, you can order them direct from Silhouette Books by sending your name, address, zip or postal code, along with a check or money order for $3.29 (ANGEL ON MY SHOULDER IM #408), and $2.79 (ANGEL FOR HIRE D #680), for each book ordered (please do not send cash), plus 75¢ postage and handling ($1.00 in Canada), payable to Silhouette Reader Service to:

In the U.S.	In Canada
3010 Walden Ave. P.O. Box 1396 Buffalo, NY 14269-1396	P.O. Box 609 Fort Erie, Ontario L2A 5X3

Please specify book title with your order.
Canadian residents add applicable federal and provincial taxes.

ANGEL